W.W. JACOBS – THE SHORT STORIES
VOLUME 9

William Wymark Jacobs was born on September 8th, 1863 in the Wapping district of London, England. Jacobs grew up near the docks, where his father was a wharf manager. The docks and river side would be a constant theme of his writing in years to come.

Although surrounded by poverty, he received a formal education in London, first at a private prep school and later at the Birkbeck Literary and Scientific Institute.

His working life began with a less than exciting clerical position at the Post Office Savings Bank. Jacobs put his imagination to good use writing short stories, sketches and articles, many for the Post Office house publication "Blackfriars Magazine."

In 1896 Jacobs published Many Cargoes, a selection of sea-faring yarns, which established him as a popular writer with a knack for authentic dialogue and trick endings.

A year later he published a novelette, The Skipper's Wooing, and in 1898 another collection of short stories; Sea Urchins. These works painted vivid pictures of dockland and seafaring London full of colourful characters.

By 1899, Jacobs was able to quit the post office and write full-time.

He married the noted suffragist Agnes Eleanor Williams (who had been jailed for her protest activities) in 1900. They set up households both in Loughton, Essex and in central London.

The publication in 1902 of At Sunwich Port and Dialstone Lane, in 1904, cemented Jacobs' reputation as one of the leading British authors of the new century.

There followed a string of further successful publications, including Captain's All (1905), Night Watches (1914), The Castaways (1916), and Sea Whispers (1926).

Though Jacobs would create little in the way of new work after 1911, he still wrote and was recognized as a leading humorist, ranked alongside such writers as P. G. Wodehouse.

William Wymark Jacobs died in a North London nursing home in Hornsey Lane, Islington on September 1st, 1943.

Index of Contents

THE RIVAL BEAUTIES

"If you hadn't asked me," said the night watchman, "I should never have told you; but, seeing as you've put the question point blank, I will tell you my experience of it. You're the first person I've ever opened my lips to upon the subject, for it was so eggstraordinary that all our chaps swore as they'd keep it to theirselves for fear of being disbelieved and jeered at.

"It happened in '84, on board the steamer George Washington, bound from Liverpool to New York. The first eight days passed without anything unusual happening, but on the ninth I was standing aft with the first mate, hauling in the log, when we hears a yell from aloft, an' a chap what we called Stuttering Sam come down as if he was possessed, and rushed up to the mate with his eyes nearly starting out of his 'ed.

"'There's the s-s-s-s-s-s-sis-sis-sip!' ses he.

"'The what?' ses the mate.

"'The s-s-sea-sea-sssssip!'

"'Look here, my lad,' ses the mate, taking out a pocket-hankerchief an' wiping his face, 'you just tarn your 'ed away till you get your breath. It's like opening a bottle o' soda water to stand talking to you. Now, what is it?'

"'It's the sssssssis-sea-sea-sea-sarpint!' ses Sam, with a bust.

"'Rather a long un by your account of it,' ses the mate, with a grin.

"'What's the matter?' ses the skipper, who just came up.

"'This man has seen the sea-sarpint, sir, that's all,' ses the mate.

"'Y-y-yes,' said Sam, with a sort o' sob.

"'Well, there ain't much doing just now,' ses the skipper, 'so you'd better get a slice o' bread and feed it.'

"The mate bust out larfing, an' I could see by the way the skipper smiled he was rather tickled at it himself.

"The skipper an' the mate was still larfing very hearty when we heard a dreadful 'owl from the bridge, an' one o' the chaps suddenly leaves the wheel, jumps on to the deck, and bolts below as though he was mad. T'other one follows 'm a'most d'reckly, and the second mate caught hold o' the wheel as he left it, and called out something we couldn't catch to the skipper.

"'What the d—'s the matter?' yells the skipper.

"The mate pointed to starboard, but as 'is 'and was shaking so that one minute it was pointing to the sky an' the next to the bottom o' the sea, it wasn't much of a guide to us. Even when he got it steady we couldn't see anything, till all of a sudden, about two miles off, something like a telegraph pole stuck up out of the water for a few seconds, and then ducked down again and made straight for the ship.

"Sam was the fust to speak, and, without wasting time stuttering or stammering, he said he'd go down and see about that bit o' bread, an' he went afore the skipper or the mate could stop 'im.

"In less than 'arf a minute there was only the three officers an' me on deck. The second mate was holding the wheel, the skipper was holding his breath, and the first mate was holding me. It was one o' the most exciting times I ever had.

"'Better fire the gun at it,' ses the skipper, in a trembling voice, looking at the little brass cannon we had for signalling.

"'Better not give him any cause for offence,' ses the mate, shaking his head.

"'I wonder whether it eats men,' ses the skipper. 'Perhaps it'll come for some of us.'

"'There ain't many on deck for it to choose from,' ses the mate, looking at 'im significant like.

"'That's true,' ses the skipper, very thoughtful; 'I'll go an' send all hands on deck. As captain, it's my duty not to leave the ship till the LAST, if I can anyways help it.'

"How he got them on deck has always been a wonder to me, but he did it. He was a brutal sort o' a man at the best o' times, an' he carried on so much that I s'pose they thought even the sarpint couldn't be worse. Anyway, up they came, an' we all stood in a crowd watching the sarpint as it came closer and closer.

"We reckoned it to be about a hundred yards long, an' it was about the most awful-looking creetur you could ever imagine. If you took all the ugliest things in the earth and mixed 'em up—gorillas an' the like— you'd only make a hangel compared to what that was. It just hung off our quarter, keeping up with us, and every now and then it would open its mouth and let us see about four yards down its throat.

"'It seems peaceable,' whispers the fust mate, arter awhile.

"'P'raps it ain't hungry,' ses the skipper. 'We'd better not let it get peckish. Try it with a loaf o' bread.'

"The cook went below and fetched up half-a-dozen, an' one o' the chaps, plucking up courage, slung it over the side, an' afore you could say 'Jack Robinson' the sarpint had woffled it up an' was looking for more. It stuck its head up and came close to the side just like the swans in Victoria Park, an' it kept that game up until it had 'ad ten loaves an' a hunk o' pork.

"'I'm afraid we're encouraging it,' ses the skipper, looking at it as it swam alongside with an eye as big as a saucer cocked on the ship.

"'P'raps it'll go away soon if we don't take no more notice of it,' ses the mate. 'Just pretend it isn't here.'

"Well, we did pretend as well as we could; but everybody hugged the port side o' the ship, and was ready to bolt down below at the shortest notice; and at last, when the beast got craning its neck up over the side as though it was looking for something, we gave it some more grub. We thought if we didn't give it he might take it, and take it off the wrong shelf, so to speak. But, as the mate said, it was encouraging it, and long arter it was dark we could hear it snorting and splashing behind us, until at last it 'ad such an effect on us the mate sent one o' the chaps down to rouse the skipper.

"'I don't think it'll do no 'arm,' ses the skipper, peering over the side, and speaking as though he knew all about sea-sarpints and their ways.

"'S'pose it puts its 'ead over the side and takes one o' the men,' ses the mate.

"'Let me know at once,' ses the skipper firmly; an' he went below agin and left us.

"Well, I was jolly glad when eight bells struck, an' I went below; an' if ever I hoped anything I hoped that when I go up that ugly brute would have gone, but, instead o' that, when I went on deck it was playing alongside like a kitten a'most, an' one o' the chaps told me as the skipper had been feeding it agin.

"'It's a wonderful animal,' ses the skipper, 'an' there's none of you now but has seen the sea-sarpint; but I forbid any man here to say a word about it when we get ashore.'

"'Why not, sir?' ses the second mate.

"'Becos you wouldn't be believed,' said the skipper sternly. 'You might all go ashore and kiss the Book an' make affidavits an' not a soul 'ud believe you. The comic papers 'ud make fun of it, and the respectable papers 'ud say it was seaweed or gulls.'

"Why not take it to New York with us?' ses the fust mate suddenly.

"'What?' ses the skipper.

"'Feed it every day,' ses the mate, getting excited, 'and bait a couple of shark hooks and keep 'em ready, together with some wire rope. Git 'im to foller us as far as he will, and then hook him. We might git him in alive and show him at a sovereign a head. Anyway, we can take in his carcase if we manage it properly.'

"'By Jove! if we only could,' ses the skipper, getting excited too.

"'We can try,' ses the mate. 'Why, we could have noosed it this mornin' if we had liked; and if it breaks the lines we must blow its head to pieces with the gun.'

"It seemed a most eggstraordinary thing to try and catch it that way; but the beast was so tame, and stuck so close to us, that it wasn't quite so ridikilous as it seemed at fust.

"Arter a couple o' days nobody minded the animal a bit, for it was about the most nervous thing of its size you ever saw. It hadn't got the soul of a mouse; and one day when the second mate, just for a lark, took the line of the foghorn in his hand and tooted it a bit, it flung up its 'ead in a scared sort o' way, and, after backing a bit, turned clean round and bolted.

"I thought the skipper 'ud have gone mad. He chucked over loaves o' bread, bits o' beef and pork, an' scores o' biskits, and by-and-bye, when the brute plucked up heart an' came arter us again, he fairly beamed with joy. Then he gave orders that nobody was to touch the horn for any reason whatever, not even if there was a fog, or chance of collision, or anything of the kind; an' he also gave orders that the bells wasn't to be struck, but that the bosen was just to shove 'is 'ead in the fo'c's'le and call 'em out instead.

"Arter three days had passed, and the thing was still follering us, everybody made certain of taking it to New York, an' I b'leeve if it hadn't been for Joe Cooper the question about the sea-sarpint would ha' been settled long ago. He was a most eggstraordinary ugly chap was Joe. He had a perfic cartoon of a face, an' he was so delikit-minded and sensitive about it that if a chap only stopped in the street and whistled as he passed him, or pointed him out to a friend, he didn't like it. He told me once when I was symperthizing with him, that the only time a woman ever spoke civilly to him was one night down Poplar way in a fog, an' he was so 'appy about it that they both walked into the canal afore he knew where they was.

"On the fourth morning, when we was only about three days from Sandy Hook, the skipper got out o' bed wrong side, an' when he went on deck he was ready to snap at anybody, an' as luck would have it, as he walked a bit forrard, he sees Joe a-sticking his phiz over the side looking at the sarpint.

"'What the d—are you doing?' shouts the skipper, 'What do you mean by it?'

"'Mean by what, sir?' asks Joe.

"'Putting your black ugly face over the side o' the ship an' frightening my sea-sarpint!' bellows the skipper, 'You know how easy it's skeered.'

"'Frightening the sea-sarpint?' ses Joe, trembling all over, an' turning very white.

"'If I see that face o' yours over the side agin, my lad,' ses the skipper very fierce, 'I'll give it a black eye. Now cut!'

"Joe cut, an' the skipper, having worked off some of his ill-temper, went aft again and began to chat with the mate quite pleasant like. I was down below at the time, an' didn't know anything about it for hours arter, and then I heard it from one o' the firemen. He comes up to me very mysterious like, an' ses, 'Bill,' he ses, 'you're a pal o' Joe's; come down here an' see what you can make of 'im.'

"Not knowing what he meant, I follered 'im below to the engine-room, an' there was Joe sitting on a bucket staring wildly in front of 'im, and two or three of 'em standing round looking at 'im with their 'eads on one side.

"'He's been like that for three hours,' ses the second engineer in a whisper, 'dazed like.'

"As he spoke Joe gave a little shudder; 'Frighten the sea-sarpint!' ses he, 'O Lord!'

"'It's turned his brain,' ses one o' the firemen, 'he keeps saying nothing but that.'

"'If we could only make 'im cry,' ses the second engineer, who had a brother what was a medical student, 'it might save his reason. But how to do it, that's the question.'

"'Speak kind to 'im, sir,' ses the fireman. 'I'll have a try if you don't mind.' He cleared his throat first, an' then he walks over to Joe and puts his hand on his shoulder an' ses very soft an' pitiful like:

"'Don't take on, Joe, don't take on, there's many a ugly mug 'ides a good 'art,'

"Afore he could think o" anything else to say, Joe ups with his fist an' gives 'im one in the ribs as nearly broke 'em. Then he turns away 'is 'ead an' shivers again, an' the old dazed look come back.

"'Joe,' I ses, shaking him, 'Joe!'

"'Frightened the sea-sarpint!' whispers Joe, staring.

"'Joe,' I ses, 'Joe. You know me, I'm your pal, Bill.'

"'Ay, ay,' ses Joe, coming round a bit.

"'Come away,' I ses, 'come an' git to bed, that's the best place for you.'

"I took 'im by the sleeve, and he gets up quiet an' obedient and follers me like a little child. I got 'im straight into 'is bunk, an' arter a time he fell into a soft slumber, an' I thought the worst had passed, but I was mistaken. He got up in three hours' time an' seemed all right, 'cept that he walked about as though he was thinking very hard about something, an' before I could make out what it was he had a fit.

"He was in that fit ten minutes, an' he was no sooner out o' that one than he was in another. In twenty-four hours he had six full-sized fits, and I'll allow I was fairly puzzled. What pleasure he could find in tumbling down hard and stiff an' kicking at everybody an' everything I couldn't see. He'd be standing quiet and peaceable like one minute, and the next he'd catch hold o' the nearest thing to him and have a bad fit, and lie on his back and kick us while we was trying to force open his hands to pat 'em.

"The other chaps said the skipper's insult had turned his brain, but I wasn't quite so soft, an' one time when he was alone I put it to him.

"'Joe, old man,' I ses, 'you an' me's been very good pals.'

"'Ay, ay,' ses he, suspicious like.

"'Joe,' I whispers, 'what's yer little game?'

"'Wodyermean?' ses he, very short.

"'I mean the fits,' ses I, looking at 'im very steady, 'It's no good looking hinnercent like that, 'cos I see yer chewing soap with my own eyes.'

"'Soap,' ses Joe, in a nasty sneering way, 'you wouldn't reckernise a piece if you saw it.'

"Arter that I could see there was nothing to be got out of 'im, an' I just kept my eyes open and watched. The skipper didn't worry about his fits, 'cept that he said he wasn't to let the sarpint see his face when he was in 'em for fear of scaring it; an' when the mate wanted to leave him out o' the watch, he ses, 'No, he might as well have fits while at work as well as anywhere else.'

"We were about twenty-four hours from port, an' the sarpint was still following us; and at six o'clock in the evening the officers puffected all their arrangements for ketching the creetur at eight o'clock next morning. To make quite sure of it an extra watch was kept on deck all night to chuck it food every half-hour; an' when I turned in at ten o'clock that night it was so close I could have reached it with a clothes-prop.

"I think I'd been abed about 'arf-an-hour when I was awoke by the most infernal row I ever heard. The foghorn was going incessantly, an' there was a lot o' shouting and running about on deck. It struck us all as 'ow the sarpint was gitting tired o' bread, and was misbehaving himself, consequently we just shoved our 'eds out o' the fore-scuttle and listened. All the hullaballoo seemed to be on the bridge, an' as we didn't see the sarpint there we plucked up courage and went on deck.

"Then we saw what had happened. Joe had 'ad another fit while at the wheel, and, NOT KNOWING WHAT HE WAS DOING, had clutched the line of the foghorn, and was holding on to it like grim death, and kicking right and left. The skipper was in his bedclothes, raving worse than Joe; and just as we got there Joe came round a bit, and, letting go o' the line, asked in a faint voice what the foghorn was blowing for. I thought the skipper 'ud have killed him; but the second mate held him back, an', of course, when things quieted down a bit, an' we went to the side, we found the sea-sarpint had vanished.

"We stayed there all that night, but it warn't no use. When day broke there wasn't the slightest trace of it, an' I think the men was as sorry to lose it as the officers. All 'cept Joe, that is, which shows how people should never be rude, even to the humblest; for I'm sartin that if the skipper hadn't hurt his feelings the way he did we should now know as much about the sea-sarpint as we do about our own brothers."

RULE OF THREE

The long summer day had gone and twilight was just merging into night. A ray of light from the lantern at the end of the quay went trembling across the sea, and in the little harbour the dusky shapes of a few small craft lay motionless on the dark water.

The master of the schooner Harebell came slowly towards the harbour, accompanied by his mate. Both men had provided ashore for a voyage which included no intoxicants, and the dignity of the skipper, always a salient feature, had developed tremendously under the influence of brown stout. He stepped aboard his schooner importantly, and then, turning to the mate, who was about to follow, suddenly held up his hand for silence.

"What did I tell you?" he inquired severely as the mate got quietly aboard.

"About knocking down the two policemen?" guessed the mate, somewhat puzzled.

"No," said the other shortly. "Listen."

The mate listened. From the foc'sle came low gruff voices of men, broken by the silvery ring of women's laughter.

"Well, I'm a Dutchman," said the mate the air of one who felt he was expected to say something.

"After all I said to 'em," said the skipper with weary dignity. "You 'eard what I said to them Jack?"

"Nobody could ha' swore louder," testified the mate.

"An' here they are," said the skipper, "defying of me. After all I said to 'em. After all the threats I—I employed."

"Employed," repeated the mate with relish.

"They've been and gone and asked them females down the foc'sle again. You know what I said I'd do, Jack, if they did."

"Said you'd eat 'em without salt," quoted the other helpfully.

"I'll do worse than that, Jack," said the skipper after a moment's discomfiture. "What's to hinder us casting off quietly and taking them along with us?

"If you ask me," said the mate, "I should think you couldn't please the crew better."

"Well, we'll see," said the other, nodding sagaciously, "don't make no noise, Jack."

He set an example of silence himself, and aided by the mate, cast off the warps which held his unconscious visitors to their native town, and the wind being off the shore the little schooner drifted silently away from the quay.

The skipper went to the wheel, and the noise of the mate hauling on the jib brought a rough head out of the foc'sle, the owner of which, after a cry to his mates below, sprang up on deck and looked round in bewilderment.

"Stand by, there!" cried the skipper as the others came rushing on deck. "Shake 'em out."

"Beggin' your pardin', sir," said one of them with more politeness in his tones than he had ever used before, "but—"

"Stand by!" said the skipper.

"Now then!" shouted the mate sharply, "lively there! Lively with it!"

The men looked at each other helplessly and went to their posts as a scream of dismay arose from the fair beings below who, having just begun to realise their position, were coming on deck to try and improve it.

"What!" roared the skipper in pretended astonishment, "what! Gells aboard after all I said? It can't be; I must be dreaming!"

"Take us back!" wailed the damsels, ignoring the sarcasm; "take us back, captain."

"No, I can't go back," said the skipper. "You see what comes o' disobedience, my gells. Lively there on that mains'l, d'ye hear?"

"We won't do it again," cried the girls, as the schooner came to the mouth of the harbour and they smelt the dark sea beyond. "Take us back."

"It can't be done," said the skipper cheerfully.

"It's agin the lor, sir," said Ephraim Biddle solemnly.

"What! Taking my own ship out?" said the skipper in affected surprise. "How was I to know they were there? I'm not going back; 'tain't likely. As they've made their beds, so they must lay on 'em."

"They ain't got no beds," said George Scott hastily. "It ain't fair to punish the gals for us, sir."

"Hold your tongue," said the skipper sharply.

"It's agin the lor, sir," said Biddle again. "If so be they're passengers, this ship ain't licensed to carry passengers. If so be as they're took out agin their will, it's abduction—I see the other day a chap had seven years for abducting one gal, three sevens—three sevens is—three sevens is—well, it's more years than you'd like to be in prison, sir."

"Bosh," said the skipper, "they're stowaways, an' I shall put 'em ashore at the first port we touch at—Plymouth."

A heartrending series of screams from the stowaways rounded his sentence, screams which gave way to sustained sobbing, as the schooner, catching the wind, began to move through the water.

"You'd better get below, my gals," said Biddle, who was the eldest member of the crew, consolingly.

"Why don't you make him take us back?" said Jenny Evans, the biggest of the three girls, indignantly.

"'Cos we can't, my dear," said Biddle reluctantly; "it's agin the lor. You don't want to see us put into prison, do you?"

"I don't mind," said Miss Evans tearfully, "so long as we get back. George, take us back."

"I can't," said Scott sullenly.

"Well, you can look for somebody else, then," said Miss Evans with temper. "You won't marry me. How much would you get if you did make the skipper put back?"

"Very likely six months," said Biddle solemnly.

"Six months would soon pass away," said Miss Evans briskly, as she wiped her eye.

"It would be a rest," said Miss Williams coaxingly.

The men not seeing things in quite the same light, they announced their intention of having nothing more to do with them, and crowding together in the bows beneath two or three blankets, condoled tearfully with each other on their misfortunes. For some time the men stood by offering clumsy consolations, but, tired at last of repeated rebuffs and insults, went below and turned in, leaving the satisfied skipper at the wheel.

The night was clear and the wind light. As the effects of his libations wore off the skipper had some misgivings as to the wisdom of his action, but it was too late to return, and he resolved to carry on.

Looking at all the circumstances of the case, he thought it best to keep the wheel in his own hands for a time, and the dawn came in the early hours and found him still at his post.

Objects began to stand out clearly in the growing light, and three dispirited girls put their heads out from their blankets and sniffed disdainfully at the sharp morning air. Then after an animated discussion they arose, and casting their blankets aside, walked up to the skipper and eyed him thoughtfully.

"As easy as easy," said Jenny Evans confidently, as she drew herself up to her full height, and looked down at the indignant man.

"Why, he isn't any bigger than a boy," said Miss Williams savagely.

"Pity we didn't think of it before," said Miss Davies. "I s'pose the crew won't help him?"

"Not they," said Miss Evans scornfully. "If they do, we'll serve them the same."

They went off, leaving the skipper a prey to gathering uneasiness, watching their movements with wrinkled brow. From the forecastle and the galley they produced two mops and a broom, and he caught his breath sharply as Miss Evans came on deck with a pot of white paint in one hand and a pot of tar in the other.

"Now, girls," said Miss Evans.

"Put those things down," said the skipper in a peremptory voice.

"Sha'n't," said Miss Evans bluntly. "You haven't got enough on yours," she said, turning to Miss Davies. "Don't spoil the skipper for a ha'porth of tar."

At this new version of an old saw they laughed joyously, and with mops dripping tar and paint on the deck, marched in military style up to the skipper, and halted in front of him, smiling wickedly.

Then the heart of the skipper waxed sore faint within him, and, with a wild yell, he summoned his trusty crew to his side.

The crew came on deck slowly, and casting furtive glances at the scene, pushed Ephraim Biddle to the front.

"Take those mops away from 'em," said the skipper haughtily.

"Don't you interfere," said Miss Evans, looking at them over her shoulder.

"Else we'll give you some," said Miss Williams bloodthirstily.

"Take those mops away from 'em!" bawled the skipper, instinctively drawing back as Miss Evans made a pass at him.

"I don't see as 'ow we can interfere, sir," said Biddle with deep respect.

"What!" said the astonished skipper.

"It would be agin the lor for us to interfere with people," said Biddle, turning to his mates, "dead agin the lor."

"Don't you talk rubbish," said the skipper anxiously. "Take 'em away from 'em. It's my tar and my paint, and—"

"You shall have it," said Miss Evans reassuringly.

"If we touched 'em," said Biddle impressively, "it'd be an assault at lor. 'Sides which, they'd probably muss us up with 'em. All we can do, sir, is to stand by and see fair play."

"Fair play!" cried the skipper dancing with rage, and turning hastily to the mate, who had just come on the scene. "Take those things away from 'em, Jack."

"Well, if it's all the same to you," said the mate, "I'd rather not be drawn into it."

"But I'd rather you were," said the skipper sharply. "Take 'em away."

"How?" inquired the mate pertinently.

"I order you to take 'em away," said the skipper. "How, is your affair."

"I'm not goin' to raise my hand against a woman for anybody," said the mate with decision. "It's no part of my work to get messed up with tar and paint from lady passengers."

"It's part of your work to obey me, though," said the skipper, raising his voice; "all of you. There's five of you, with the mate, and only three gells. What are you afraid of?"

"Are you going to take us back?" demanded Jenny Evans.

"Run away," said the skipper with dignity. "Run away."

"I shall ask you three times," said Miss Evans sternly. "One—are you going back? Two—are you going back? Three—"

In the midst of a breathless silence she drew within striking distance, while her allies, taking up a position on either flank of the enemy, listened attentively to the instructions of their leader.

"Be careful he doesn't catch hold of the mops," said Miss Evans; "but if he does, the others are to hit him over the head with the handles. Never mind about hurting him."

"Take this wheel a minnit, Jack," said the skipper, pale but determined.

The mate came forward and took it unwillingly, and the skipper, trying hard to conceal his trepidation, walked towards Miss Evans and tried to quell her with his eye. The power of the human eye is notorious, and Miss Evans showed her sense of the danger she ran by making an energetic attempt to close the skipper's with her mop, causing him to duck with amazing nimbleness. At the same moment another mop loaded with white paint was pushed into the back of his neck. He turned with a cry of rage, and then realising the odds against him flung his dignity to the winds and dodged with the agility of a schoolboy. Through the galley and round the masts he went with the avenging mops in mad pursuit, until breathless and exhausted he suddenly sprang on to the side and climbed frantically into the rigging.

"Coward!" said Miss Evans, shaking her weapon at him.

"Come down," cried Miss Williams. "Come down like a man."

"It's no good wasting time over him," said Miss Evans, after another vain appeal to the skipper's manhood. "He's escaped. Get some more stuff on your mops."

The mate, who had been laughing boisterously, checked himself suddenly, and assumed a gravity of demeanour more in accordance with his position. The mops were dipped in solemn silence, and Miss Evans approaching regarded him significantly.

"Now, my dears," said the mate, waving his hand with a deprecatory gesture, "don't be silly."

"Don't be what?" inquired the sensitive Miss Evans, raising her mop.

"You know what I mean," said the mate hastily. "I can't help myself."

"Well, we're going to help you," said Miss Evans. "Turn the ship round."

"You obey orders, Jack," cried the skipper from aloft.

"It's all very well for you sitting up there in peace and comfort," said the mate indignantly. "I'm not going to be tarred to please you. Come down and take charge of your ship."

"Do your duty, Jack," said the skipper, who was polishing his face with a handkerchief. "They won't touch you. They daren't. They're afraid to."

"You're egging 'em on," cried the mate wrathfully. "I won't steer; come and take it yourself."

He darted behind the wheel as Miss Evans, who was getting impatient, made a thrust at him, and then, springing out, gained the side and rushed up the rigging after his captain. Biddle, who was standing close by, gazed earnestly at them and took the wheel.

"You won't hurt old Biddle, I know," he said, trying to speak confidently.

"Of course not," said Miss Evans emphatically.

"Tar don't hurt," explained Miss Williams.

"It's good for you," said the third lady positively. "One—two—"

"It's no good," said the mate as Ephraim came suddenly into the rigging; "you'll have to give in."

"I'm damned if I will," said the infuriated skipper. Then an idea occurred to him, and puckering his face shrewdly he began to descend.

"All right," he said shortly, as Miss Evans advanced to receive him. "I'll go back."

He took the wheel; the schooner came round before the wind, and the willing crew, letting the sheets go, hauled them in again on the port side.

"And now, my lads," said the skipper with a benevolent smile, "just clear that mess up off the decks, and you may as well pitch them mops overboard. They'll never be any good again."

He spoke carelessly, albeit his voice trembled a little, but his heart sank within him as Miss Evans, with a horrible contortion of her pretty face, intended for a wink, waved them back.

"You stay where you are," she said imperiously; "we'll throw them overboard—when we've done with them. What did you say, captain?"

The skipper was about to repeat it with great readiness when Miss Evans raised her trusty mop. The words died away on his lips, and after a hopeless glance from his mate to the crew and from the crew to the rigging, he accepted his defeat, and in grim silence took them home again.

SAM'S BOY

It was getting late in the afternoon as Master Jones, in a somewhat famished condition, strolled up Aldgate, with a keen eye on the gutter, in search of anything that would serve him for his tea. Too late, he wished that he had saved some of the stale bread and damaged fruit which had constituted his dinner.

Aldgate proving barren, he turned up into the quieter Minories, skilfully dodging the mechanical cuff of the constable at the corner as he passed, and watching with some interest the efforts of a stray mongrel to get itself adopted. Its victim had sworn at it, cut at it with his stick, and even made little runs at it—all to no purpose. Finally, being a soft-hearted man, he was weak enough to pat the cowering schemer on the head, and, being frantically licked by the homeless one, took it up in his arms and walked off with it.

Billy Jones watched the proceedings with interest, not untempered by envy. If he had only been a dog! The dog passed in the man's arms, and, with a whine of ecstasy, insisted upon licking his ear. They went on their way, the dog wondering between licks what sort of table the man kept, and the man speculating idly as to a descent which appeared to have included, among other things, an ant-eater.

"'E's all right," said the orphan, wistfully; "no coppers to chivvy 'im about, and as much grub as he wants. Wish I'd been a dog."

He tied up his breeches with a piece of string which was lying on the pavement, and, his hands being now free, placed them in a couple of rents which served as pockets, and began to whistle. He was not a proud boy, and was quite willing to take a lesson even from the humblest. Surely he was as useful as a dog!

The thought struck him just as a stout, kindly-looking seaman passed with a couple of shipmates. It was a good-natured face, and the figure was that of a man who lived well. A moment's hesitation, and Master Jones, with a courage born of despair, ran after him and tugged him by the sleeve.

"Halloa!" said Mr. Samuel Brown, looking round. "What do you want?"

"Want you, father," said Master Jones.

The jolly seaman's face broke into a smile. So also did the faces of the jolly seaman's friends.

"I'm not your father, matey," he said, good-naturedly.

"Yes, you are," said the desperate Billy; "you know you are."

"You've made a mistake, my lad," said Mr. Brown, still smiling. "Here, run away."

He felt in his trouser pocket and produced a penny. It was a gift, not a bribe, but it had by no means the effect its donor intended. Master Jones, now quite certain that he had made a wise choice of a father, trotted along a yard or two in the rear.

"Look here, my lad," exclaimed Mr. Brown, goaded into action by intercepting a smile with which Mr. Charles Legge had favoured Mr. Harry Green, "you run off home."

"Where do you live now?" inquired Billy, anxiously.

Mr. Green, disdaining concealment, slapped Mr. Legge on the back, and, laughing uproariously, regarded Master Jones with much kindness.

"You mustn't follow me," said Sam, severely; "d'ye hear?"

"All right, father," said the boy, dutifully.

"And don't call me father," vociferated Mr. Brown.

"Why not?" inquired the youth, artlessly.

Mr. Legge stopped suddenly, and, putting his hand on Mr. Green's shoulder, gaspingly expressed his inability to go any farther. Mr. Green, patting his back, said he knew how he felt, because he felt the same, and, turning to Sam, told him he'd be the death of him if he wasn't more careful.

"If you don't run away," said Mr. Brown, harshly, as he turned to the boy, "I shall give you a hiding."

"Where am I to run to?" whimpered Master Jones, dodging off and on.

"Run 'ome," said Sam.

"That's where I'm going," said Master Jones, following.

"Better try and give 'im the slip, Sam," said Mr. Legge, in a confidential whisper; "though it seems an unnatural thing to do."

"Unnatural? What d'ye mean?" demanded his unfortunate friend. "Wot d'ye mean by unnatural?"

"Oh, if you're going to talk like that, Sam," said Mr. Legge, shortly, "it's no good giving you advice. As you've made your bed, you must lay on it."

"How long is it since you saw 'im last, matey?" inquired Mr. Green.

"I dunno; not very long," replied the boy, cautiously.

"Has he altered at all since you see 'im last?" inquired the counsel for the defence, motioning the fermenting Mr. Brown to keep still.

"No," said Billy, firmly; "not a bit."

"Wot's your name?"

"Billy," was the reply.

"Billy wot?"

"Billy Jones."

Mr. Green's face cleared, and he turned to his friends with a smile of joyous triumph. Sam's face reflected his own, but Charlie Legge's was still overcast.

"It ain't likely," he said impressively; "it ain't likely as Sam would go and get married twice in the same name, is it? Put it to yourself, 'Arry—would you?

"Look 'ere," exclaimed the infuriated Mr. Brown, "don't you interfere in my business. You're a crocodile, that's wot you are. As for you, you little varmint, you run off, d'ye hear?"

He moved on swiftly, accompanied by the other two, and set an example of looking straight ahead of him, which was, however, lost upon his friends.

"'E's still following of you, Sam," said the crocodile, in by no means disappointed tones.

"Sticking like a leech," confirmed Mr. Green. "'E's a pretty little chap, rather."

"Takes arter 'is mother," said the vengeful Mr. Legge.

The unfortunate Sam said nothing, but strode a haunted man down Nightingale Lane into Wapping High Street, and so to the ketch Nancy Bell, which was lying at Shrimpett's Wharf. He stepped on board without a word, and only when he turned to descend the forecastle ladder did his gaze rest for a moment on the small, forlorn piece of humanity standing on the wharf.

"Halloa, boy, what do you want?" cried the skipper, catching sight of him.

"Want my father, sir—Sam," replied the youth, who had kept his ears open.

The skipper got up from his seat and eyed him curiously; Messrs. Legge and Green, drawing near, explained the situation. Now the skipper was a worldly man; and Samuel Brown, A.B., when at home, played a brass instrument in the Salvation Army band. He regarded the boy kindly and spoke to him fair.

"Don't run away," he said, anxiously.

"I'm not going to, sir," said Master Jones, charmed with his manner, and he watched breathlessly as the skipper stepped forward, and, peering down the forecastle, called loudly for Sam.

"Yes, sir," said a worried voice.

"Your boy's asking after you," said the skipper, grinning madly.

"He's not my boy, sir," replied Mr. Brown, through his clenched teeth.

"Well, you'd better come up and see him," said the other. "Are you sure he isn't, Sam?"

Mr. Brown made no reply, but coming on deck met Master Jones's smile of greeting with an icy stare, and started convulsively as the skipper beckoned him aboard.

"He's been rather neglected, Sam," said the skipper, shaking his head.

"Wot's it got to do with me?" said Sam, violently. "I tell you I've never seen 'im afore this arternoon."

"You hear what your father says," said the skipper—("Hold your tongue, Sam.) Where's your mother, boy?"

"Dead, sir," whined Master Jones. "I've on'y got 'im now."

The skipper was a kind-hearted man, and he looked pityingly at the forlorn little figure by his side. And Sam was the good man of the ship and a leading light at Dimport.

"How would you like to come to sea with your father?" he inquired.

The grin of delight with which Master Jones received this proposal was sufficient reply.

"I wouldn't do it for everybody," pursued the skipper, glancing severely at the mate, who was behaving foolishly, "but I don't mind obliging you, Sam. He can come."

"Obliging?" repeated Mr. Brown, hardly able to get the words out. "Obliging me? I don't want to be obliged."

"There, there," interrupted the skipper. "I don't want any thanks. Take him forrard and give him something to eat—he looks half-starved, poor little chap."

He turned away and went down to the cabin, while the cook, whom Mr. Brown had publicly rebuked for his sins the day before, led the boy to the galley and gave him a good meal. After that was done Charlie washed him, and Harry going ashore, begged a much-worn suit of boy's clothes from a foreman of his acquaintance. He also brought back a message from the foreman to Mr. Brown to the effect that he was surprised at him.

The conversation that evening after Master Jones was asleep turned upon bigamy, but Mr. Brown snored through it all, though Mr. Legge's remark that the revelations of that afternoon had thrown a light upon many little things in his behaviour which had hitherto baffled him came perilously near to awaking him.

At six in the morning they got under way, the boy going nearly frantic with delight as sail after sail was set, and the ketch, with a stiff breeze, rapidly left London behind her. Mr. Brown studiously ignored him, but the other men pampered him to his heart's content, and even the cabin was good enough to manifest a little concern in his welfare, the skipper calling Mr. Brown up no fewer than five times that day to complain about his son's behaviour.

"I can't have somersaults on this 'ere ship, Sam," he remarked, shaking his head; "it ain't the place for 'em."

"I wonder at you teaching 'im such things," said the mate, in grave disapprobation.

"Me?" said the hapless Sam, trembling with passion.

"He must 'ave seen you do it," said the mate, letting his eye rove casually over Sam's ample proportions. "You must ha' been leading a double life altogether, Sam."

"That's nothing to do with us," interrupted the skipper, impatiently. "I don't mind Sam turning cart-wheels all day if it amuses him, but they mustn't do it here, that's all. It's no good standing there sulking, Sam; I can't have it."

He turned away, and Mr. Brown, unable to decide whether he was mad or drunk, or both, walked back, and, squeezing himself up in the bows, looked miserably over the sea. Behind him the men disported themselves with Master Jones, and once, looking over his shoulder, he actually saw the skipper giving him a lesson in steering.

By the following afternoon he was in such a state of collapse that, when they put in at the small port of Withersea to discharge a portion of their cargo, he obtained permission to stay below in his bunk. Work proceeded without him, and at nine o'clock in the evening they sailed again, and it was not until they were a couple of miles on their way to Dimport that Mr. Legge rushed aft with the announcement that he was missing.

"Don't talk nonsense," said the skipper, as he came up from below in response to a hail from the mate.

"It's a fact, sir," said Mr. Legge, shaking his head.

"What's to be done with the boy?" demanded the mate, blankly.

"Sam's a unsteady, unreliable, tricky old man," exclaimed the skipper, hotly; "the idea of going and leaving a boy on our hands like that. I'm surprised at him. I'm disappointed in Sam—deserting!"

"I expect 'e's larfing like anything, sir," remarked Mr. Legge.

"Get forrard," said the skipper, sharply; "get forrard at once, d'ye hear?"

"But what's to be done with the boy?—that's what I want to know," said the mate.

"What d'ye think's to be done with him?" bawled the skipper. "We can't chuck him overboard, can we?"

"I mean when we get to Dimport?" growled the mate.

"Well, the men'll talk," said the skipper, calming down a little, "and perhaps Sam's wife'll come and take him. If not, I suppose he'll have to go to the workhouse. Anyway, it's got nothing to do with me. I wash my hands of it altogether."

He went below again, leaving the mate at the wheel. A murmur of voices came from the forecastle, where the crew were discussing the behaviour of their late colleague. The bereaved Master Jones, whose face was streaky with the tears of disappointment, looked on from his bunk.

"What are you going to do, Billy?" inquired the cook.

"I dunno," said the boy, miserably.

He sat up in his bunk in a brown study, ever and anon turning his sharp little eyes from one to another of the men. Then, with a final sniff to the memory of his departed parent, he composed himself to sleep.

With the buoyancy of childhood he had forgotten his trouble by the morning, and ran idly about the ship as before, until in the afternoon they came in sight of Dimport. Mr. Legge, who had a considerable respect for the brain hidden in that small head, pointed it out to him, and with some curiosity waited for his remarks.

"I can see it," said Master Jones, briefly.

"That's where Sam lives," said his friend, pointedly.

"Yes," said the boy, nodding, "all of you live there, don't you?"

It was an innocent enough remark in all conscience, but there was that in Master Jones's eye which caused Mr. Legge to move away hastily and glance at him in some disquietude from the other side of the deck. The boy, unconscious of the interest excited by his movements, walked restlessly up and down.

"Boy's worried," said the skipper, aside, to the mate; "cheer up, sonny."

Billy looked up and smiled, and the cloud which had sat on his brow when he thought of the coldblooded desertion of Mr. Brown gave way to an expression of serene content.

"Well, what's he going to do?" inquired the mate, in a low voice.

"That needn't worry us," said the skipper.

"Let things take their course; that's my motto."

He took the wheel from Harry; the little town came closer; the houses separated and disclosed roads, and the boy discovered to his disappointment that the church stood on ground of its own, and not on the roof of a large red house as he had supposed. He ran forward as they got closer, and, perching up in the bows until they were fast to the quay, looked round searchingly for any signs of Sam.

The skipper locked up the cabin, and then calling on one of the shore hands to keep an eye on the forecastle, left it open for the convenience of the small passenger. Harry, Charlie, and the cook stepped ashore. The skipper and mate followed, and the latter, looking back from some distance, called his attention to the desolate little figure sitting on the hatch.

"I s'pose he'll be all right," said the skipper, uneasily; "there's food and a bed down the fo'c's'le. You might just look round to-night and see he's safe. I expect we'll have to take him back to London with us."

They turned up a small road in the direction of home and walked on in silence, until the mate, glancing behind at an acquaintance who had just passed, uttered a sharp exclamation. The skipper turned, and a small figure which had just shot round the corner stopped in mid-career and eyed them warily. The men exchanged uneasy glances.

"Father," cried a small voice.

"He—he's adopted you now," said the skipper, huskily.

"Or you," said the mate. "I never took much notice of him."

He looked round again. Master Jones was following briskly, about ten yards in the rear, and twenty yards behind him came the crew, who, having seen him quit the ship, had followed with the evident intention of being in at the death.

"Father," cried the boy again, "wait for me."

One or two passers-by stared in astonishment, and the mate began to be uneasy as to the company he was keeping.

"Let's separate," he growled, "and see who he's calling after."

The skipper caught him by the arm. "Shout out to him to go back," he cried.

"It's you he's after, I tell you," said the mate. "Who do you want, Billy?"

"I want my father," cried the youth, and, to prevent any mistake, indicated the raging skipper with his finger.

"Who do you want?" bellowed the latter, in a frightful voice.

"Want you, father," chirrupped Master Jones.

Wrath and dismay struggled for supremacy in the skipper's face, and he paused to decide whether it would be better to wipe Master Jones off the face of the earth or to pursue his way in all the strength of conscious innocence. He chose the latter course, and, a shade more erect than usual, walked on until he came in sight of his house and his wife, who was standing at the door.

"You come along o' me, Jem, and explain," he whispered to the mate. Then he turned about and hailed the crew. The crew, flattered at being offered front seats in the affair, came forward eagerly.

"What's the matter?" inquired Mrs. Hunt, eyeing the crowd in amazement as it grouped itself in anticipation.

"Nothing," said her husband, off-handedly.

"Who's that boy?" cried the innocent woman.

"It's a poor little mad boy," began the skipper; "he came aboard—"

"I'm not mad, father," interrupted Master Jones.

"A poor little mad boy," continued the skipper, hastily, "who came aboard in London and said poor old Sam Brown was his father."

"No—you, father," cried the boy, shrilly.

"He calls everybody his father," said the skipper, with a smile of anguish; "that's the form his madness takes. He called Jem here his father."

"No, he didn't," said the mate, bluntly.

"And then he thought Charlie was his father."

"No, sir," said Mr. Legge, with respectful firmness.

"Well, he said Sam Brown was," said the skipper.

"Yes, that's right, sir," said the crew. "Where is Sam?" inquired Mrs. Hunt, looking round expectantly.

"He deserted the ship at Withersea," said her husband.

"I see," said Mrs. Hunt, with a bitter smile, "and these men have all come up prepared to swear that the boy said Sam was his father. Haven't you?"

"Yes, mum," chorused the crew, delighted at being understood so easily.

Mrs. Hunt looked across the road to the fields stretching beyond. Then she suddenly brought her gaze back, and, looking full at her husband, uttered just two words—

"Oh, Joe!"

"Ask the mate," cried the frantic skipper.

"Yes, I know what the mate'll say," said Mrs. Hunt. "I've no need to ask him."

"Charlie and Harry were with Sam when the boy came up to them," protested the skipper.

"I've no doubt," said his wife. "Oh, Joe! Joe! Joe!"

There was an uncomfortable silence, during which the crew, standing for the most part on one leg in sympathy with their chief's embarrassment, nudged each other to say something to clear the character of a man whom all esteemed.

"You ungrateful little devil," burst out Mr. Legge, at length; "arter the kind way the skipper treated you, too."

"Did he treat him kindly?" inquired the captain's wife, in conversational tones.

"Like a fa—like a uncle, mum," said the thoughtless Mr. Legge. "Gave 'im a passage on the ship and fairly spoilt 'im. We was all surprised at the fuss 'e made of 'im; wasn't we, Harry?"

He turned to his friend, but on Mr. Green's face there was an expression of such utter scorn and contempt that his own fell. He glanced at the skipper, and was almost frightened at his appearance.

The situation was ended by Mrs. Hunt entering the house and closing the door with an ominous bang. The men slunk off, headed by Mr. Legge; and the mate, after a few murmured words of encouragement to the skipper, also departed. Captain Hunt looked first at the small cause of his trouble, who had drawn off to some distance, and then at the house. Then, with a determined gesture, he turned the handle of the door and walked in. His wife, who was sitting in an armchair, with her eyes on the floor, remained motionless.

"Look here, Polly—," he began.

"Don't talk to me," was the reply. "I wonder you can look me in the face."

The skipper ground his teeth, and strove to maintain an air of judicial calm.

"If you'll only be reasonable—," he remarked, severely.

"I thought there was something secret going on," said Mrs. Hunt. "I've often looked at you when you've been sitting in that chair, with a worried look on your face, and wondered what it was. But I never thought it was so bad as this. I'll do you the credit to say that I never thought of such a thing as this.... What did you say?... What?"

"I said 'damn!'" said the skipper, explosively.

"Yes, I've no doubt," said his wife, fiercely. "You think you're going to carry it off with a high hand and bluster; but you won't bluster me, my man. I'm not one of your meek and mild women who'll put up with anything. I'm not one of your—"

"I tell you," said the skipper, "that the boy calls everybody his father. I dare say he's claimed another by this time."

Even as he spoke the handle turned, and the door opening a few inches disclosed the anxious face of Master Jones. Mrs. Hunt, catching the skipper's eye, pointed to it in an ecstasy of silent wrath. There was a breathless pause, broken at last by the boy.

"Mother!" he said, softly.

Mrs. Hunt stiffened in her chair and her arms fell by her side as she gazed in speechless amazement. Master Jones, opening the door a little wider, gently insinuated his small figure into the room. The skipper gave one glance at his wife and then, turning hastily away, put his hand over his mouth, and, with protruding eyes, gazed out of the window.

"Mother, can I come in?" said the boy.

"Oh, Polly!" sighed the skipper. Mrs. Hunt strove to regain the utterance of which astonishment had deprived her.

"I... what... Joe... don't be a fool!"

"Yes, I've no doubt," said the skipper, theatrically. "Oh, Polly! Polly! Polly!"

He put his hand over his mouth again and laughed silently, until his wife, coming behind him, took him by the shoulders and shook him violently.

"This," said the skipper, choking; "this is what—you've been worried about—This is the secret what's—"

He broke off suddenly as his wife thrust him by main force into a chair, and standing over him with a fiery face dared him to say another word. Then she turned to the boy.

"What do you mean by calling me 'mother'?" she demanded. "I'm not your mother."

"Yes, you are," said Master Jones.

Mrs. Hunt eyed him in bewilderment, and then, roused to a sense of her position by a renewed gurgling from the skipper's chair, set to work to try and thump that misguided man into a more serious frame of mind. Failing in this, she sat down, and, after a futile struggle, began to laugh herself, and that so heartily that Master Jones, smiling sympathetically, closed the door and came boldly into the room.

The statement, generally believed, that Captain Hunt and his wife adopted him, is incorrect, the skipper accounting for his continued presence in the house by the simple explanation that he had adopted them. An explanation which Mr. Samuel Brown, for one, finds quite easy of acceptance.

SAM'S GHOST

Yes, I know, said the night-watchman, thoughtfully, as he sat with a cold pipe in his mouth gazing across the river. I've 'eard it afore. People tell me they don't believe in ghosts and make a laugh of 'em, and all I say is: let them take on a night-watchman's job. Let 'em sit 'ere all alone of a night with the water lapping against the posts and the wind moaning in the corners; especially if a pal of theirs has slipped overboard, and there is little nasty bills stuck up just outside in the High Street offering a reward for the body. Twice men 'ave fallen overboard from this jetty, and I've 'ad to stand my watch here the same night, and not a farthing more for it.

One of the worst and artfullest ghosts I ever 'ad anything to do with was Sam Bullet. He was a waterman at the stairs near by 'ere; the sort o' man that 'ud get you to pay for drinks, and drink yours up by mistake arter he 'ad finished his own. The sort of man that 'ad always left his baccy-box at 'ome, but always 'ad a big pipe in 'is pocket.

He fell overboard off of a lighter one evening, and all that his mates could save was 'is cap. It was on'y two nights afore that he 'ad knocked down an old man and bit a policeman's little finger to the bone, so that, as they pointed out to the widder, p'r'aps he was taken for a wise purpose. P'r'aps he was 'appier where he was than doing six months.

"He was the sort o' chap that'll make himself 'appy anywhere," ses one of 'em, comforting-like.

"Not without me," ses Mrs. Bullet, sobbing, and wiping her eyes on something she used for a pocket-hankercher. "He never could bear to be away from me. Was there no last words?"

"On'y one," ses one o' the chaps, Joe Peel by name.

"As 'e fell overboard," ses the other.

Mrs. Bullet began to cry agin, and say wot a good 'usband he 'ad been. "Seventeen years come Michaelmas," she ses, "and never a cross word. Nothing was too good for me. Nothing. I 'ad only to ask to 'ave."

"Well, he's gorn now," ses Joe, "and we thought we ought to come round and tell you."

"So as you can tell the police," ses the other chap.

That was 'ow I came to hear of it fust; a policeman told me that night as I stood outside the gate 'aving a quiet pipe. He wasn't shedding tears; his only idea was that Sam 'ad got off too easy.

"Well, well," I ses, trying to pacify 'im, "he won't bite no more fingers; there's no policemen where he's gorn to."

He went off grumbling and telling me to be careful, and I put my pipe out and walked up and down the wharf thinking. On'y a month afore I 'ad lent Sam fifteen shillings on a gold watch and chain wot he said an uncle 'ad left 'im. I wasn't wearing it because 'e said 'is uncle wouldn't like it, but I 'ad it in my pocket, and I took it out under one of the lamps and wondered wot I ought to do.

My fust idea was to take it to Mrs. Bullet, and then, all of a sudden, the thought struck me: "Suppose he 'adn't come by it honest?"

I walked up and down agin, thinking. If he 'adn't, and it was found out, it would blacken his good name and break 'is pore wife's 'art. That's the way I looked at it, and for his sake and 'er sake I determined to stick to it.

I felt 'appier in my mind when I 'ad decided on that, and I went round to the Bear's Head and 'ad a pint. Arter that I 'ad another, and then I come back to the wharf and put the watch and chain on and went on with my work.

Every time I looked down at the chain on my waistcoat it reminded me of Sam. I looked on to the river and thought of 'im going down on the ebb. Then I got a sort o' lonesome feeling standing on the end of the jetty all alone, and I went back to the Bear's Head and 'ad another pint.

They didn't find the body, and I was a'most forgetting about Sam when one evening, as I was sitting on a box waiting to get my breath back to 'ave another go at sweeping, Joe Peel, Sam's mate, came on to the wharf to see me.

He came in a mysterious sort o' way that I didn't like: looking be'ind 'im as though he was afraid of being follered, and speaking in a whisper as if 'e was afraid of being heard. He wasn't a man I liked, and I was glad that the watch and chain was stowed safe away in my trowsis-pocket.

"I've 'ad a shock, watchman," he ses.

"Oh!" I ses.

"A shock wot's shook me all up," he ses, working up a shiver. "I've seen something wot I thought people never could see, and wot I never want to see agin. I've seen Sam!"

I thought a bit afore I spoke. "Why, I thought he was drownded," I ses.

"So 'e is," ses Joe. "When I say I've seen 'im I mean that I 'ave seen his ghost!"

He began to shiver agin, all over.

"Wot was it like?" I ses, very calm.

"Like Sam," he ses, rather short.

"When was it?" I ses.

"Last night at a quarter to twelve," he ses. "It was standing at my front door waiting for me."

"And 'ave you been shivering like that ever since?" I ses.

"Worse than that," ses Joe, looking at me very 'ard. "It's wearing off now. The ghost gave me a message for you."

I put my 'and in my trowsis-pocket and looked at 'im. Then I walked very slow, towards the gate.

"It gave me a message for you," ses Joe, walking beside me. "'We was always pals, Joe,'" it ses, "'you and me, and I want you to pay up fifteen bob for me wot I borrowed off of Bill the watchman. I can't rest until it's paid,' it ses. So here's the fifteen bob, watchman."

He put his 'and in 'is pocket and takes out fifteen bob and 'olds it out to me.

"No, no," I ses. "I can't take your money, Joe Peel. It wouldn't be right. Pore Sam is welcome to the fifteen bob—I don't want it."

"You must take it," ses Joe. "The ghost said if you didn't it would come to me agin and agin till you did, and I can't stand any more of it."

"I can't 'elp your troubles," I ses.

"You must," ses Joe. "'Give Bill the fifteen bob,' it ses, 'and he'll give you a gold watch and chain wot I gave 'im to mind till it was paid.'"

I see his little game then. "Gold watch and chain," I ses, laughing. "You must ha' misunderstood it, Joe."

"I understood it right enough," ses Joe, getting a bit closer to me as I stepped outside the gate. "Here's your fifteen bob; are you going to give me that watch and chain?"

"Sartainly not," I ses. "I don't know wot you mean by a watch and chain. If I 'ad it and I gave it to anybody, I should give it to Sam's widder, not to you."

"It's nothing to do with 'er," ses Joe, very quick. "Sam was most pertikler about that."

"I expect you dreamt it all," I ses. "Where would pore Sam get a gold watch and chain from? And why should 'e go to you about it? Why didn't 'e come to me? If 'e thinks I 'ave got it let 'im come to me."

"All right, I'll go to the police-station," ses Joe.

"I'll come with you," I ses. "But 'ere's a policeman coming along. Let's go to 'im."

I moved towards 'im, but Joe hung back, and, arter using one or two words that would ha' made any ghost ashamed to know 'im, he sheered off. I 'ad a word or two with the policeman about the weather, and then I went inside and locked the gate.

My idea was that Sam 'ad told Joe about the watch and chain afore he fell overboard. Joe was a nasty customer, and I could see that I should 'ave to be a bit careful. Some men might ha' told the police about it—but I never cared much for them. They're like kids in a way, always asking questions—most of which you can't answer.

It was a little bit creepy all alone on the wharf that night. I don't deny it. Twice I thought I 'eard something coming up on tip-toe behind me. The second time I was so nervous that I began to sing to keep my spirits up, and I went on singing till three of the hands of the Susan Emily, wot was lying alongside, came up from the fo'c'sle and offered to fight me. I was thankful when daylight came.

Five nights arterwards I 'ad the shock of my life. It was the fust night for some time that there was no craft up. A dark night, and a nasty moaning sort of a wind. I 'ad just lighted the lamp at the corner of the warehouse, wot 'ad blown out, and was sitting down to rest afore putting the ladder away, when I 'appened to look along the jetty and saw a head coming up over the edge of it. In the light of the lamp I saw the dead white face of Sam Bullet's ghost making faces at me.

I just caught my breath, sharp like, and then turned and ran for the gate like a race-horse. I 'ad left the key in the padlock, in case of anything happening, and I just gave it one turn, flung the wicket open and slammed it in the ghost's face, and tumbled out into the road.

I ran slap into the arms of a young policeman wot was passing. Nasty, short-tempered chap he was, but I don't think I was more glad to see anybody in my life. I hugged 'im till 'e nearly lost 'is breath, and then he sat me down on the kerb-stone and asked me wot I meant by it.

Wot with the excitement and the running I couldn't speak at fust, and when I did he said I was trying to deceive 'im.

"There ain't no such thing as ghosts," he ses; "you've been drinking."

"It came up out o' the river and run arter me like the wind," I ses.

"Why didn't it catch you, then?" he ses, looking me up and down and all round about. "Talk sense."

He went up to the gate and peeped in, and, arter watching a moment, stepped inside and walked down the wharf, with me follering. It was my dooty; besides, I didn't like being left all alone by myself.

Twice we walked up and down and all over the wharf. He flashed his lantern into all the dark corners, into empty barrels and boxes, and then he turned and flashed it right into my face and shook his 'ead at me.

"You've been having a bit of a lark with me," he ses, "and for two pins I'd take you. Mind, if you say a word about this to anybody, I will."

He stalked off with his 'ead in the air, and left me all alone in charge of a wharf with a ghost on it. I stayed outside in the street, of course, but every now and then I fancied I heard something moving about the other side of the gate, and once it was so distinct that I run along to the Bear's Head and knocked 'em up and asked them for a little brandy, for illness.

I didn't get it, of course; I didn't expect to; but I 'ad a little conversation with the landlord from 'is bedroom-winder that did me more good than the brandy would ha' done. Once or twice I thought he would 'ave fallen out, and many a man has 'ad his licence taken away for less than a quarter of wot 'e said to me that night. Arter he thought he 'ad finished and was going back to bed agin, I pointed' out to 'im that he 'adn't kissed me "good night," and if it 'adn't ha' been for 'is missis and two grown-up daughters and the potman I believe he'd ha' talked to me till daylight.

'Ow I got through the rest of the night I don't know. It seemed to be twenty nights instead of one, but the day came at last, and when the hands came on at six o'clock they found the gate open and me on dooty same as usual.

I slept like a tired child when I got 'ome, and arter a steak and onions for dinner I sat down and lit my pipe and tried to think wot was to be done. One thing I was quite certain about: I wasn't going to spend another night on that wharf alone.

I went out arter a bit, as far as the Clarendon Arms, for a breath of fresh air, and I 'ad just finished a pint and was wondering whether I ought to 'ave another, when Ted Dennis came in, and my mind was made up. He 'ad been in the Army all 'is life, and, so far, he 'ad never seen anything that 'ad frightened 'im. I've seen him myself take on men twice 'is size just for the love of the thing, and, arter knocking them silly, stand 'em a pint out of 'is own pocket. When I asked 'im whether he was afraid of ghosts he laughed so 'ard that the landlord came from the other end of the bar to see wot was the matter.

I stood Ted a pint, and arter he 'ad finished it I told 'im just how things was. I didn't say anything about the watch and chain, because there was no need to, and when we came outside agin I 'ad engaged an assistant-watchman for ninepence a night.

"All you've got to do," I ses, "is to keep me company. You needn't turn up till eight o'clock of a night, and you can leave 'arf an hour afore me in the morning."

"Right-o!" ses Ted. "And if I see the ghost I'll make it wish it 'ad never been born."

It was a load off my mind, and I went 'ome and ate a tea that made my missis talk about the work-'ouse, and orstritches in 'uman shape wot would eat a woman out of 'ouse and 'ome if she would let 'em.

I got to the wharf just as it was striking six, and at a quarter to seven the wicket was pushed open gentle and the ugly 'ead of Mr. Joe Peel was shoved inside.

"Hullo!" I ses. "Wot do you want?"

"I want to save your life," he ses, in a solemn voice. "You was within a inch of death last night, watchman."

"Oh!" I ses, careless-like. "'Ow do you know!"

"The ghost o' Sam Bullet told me," ses Joe. "Arter it 'ad chased you up the wharf screaming for 'elp, it came round and told me all about it."

"It seems fond of you," I ses. "I wonder why?"

"It was in a terrible temper," ses Joe, "and its face was awful to look at. 'Tell the watchman,' it ses, 'that if he don't give you the watch and chain I shall appear to 'im agin and kill 'im.'"

"All right," I ses, looking behind me to where three of the 'ands of the Daisy was sitting on the fo'c'sle smoking. "I've got plenty of company to-night."

"Company won't save you," ses Joe. "For the last time, are you going to give me that watch and chain, or not? Here's your fifteen bob."

"No," I ses; "even if I 'ad got it I shouldn't give it to you; and it's no use givin' it to the ghost, because, being made of air, he 'asn't got anywhere to put it."

"Very good," ses Joe, giving me a black look. "I've done all I can to save you, but if you won't listen to sense, you won't. You'll see Sam Bullet agin, and you'll not on'y lose the watch and chain but your life as well."

"All right," I ses, "and thank you kindly, but I've got an assistant, as it 'appens—a man wot wants to see a ghost."

"An' assistant?" ses Joe, staring.

"An old soldier," I ses. "A man wot likes trouble and danger. His idea is to shoot the ghost and see wot 'appens."

"Shoot!" ses Joe. "Shoot a pore 'armless ghost. Does he want to be 'ung? Ain't it enough for a pore man to be drownded, but wot you must try and shoot 'im arterwards? Why, you ought to be ashamed o' yourself. Where's your 'art?"

"It won't be shot if it don't come on my wharf," I ses. "Though I don't mind if it does when I've got somebody with me. I ain't afraid of anything living, and I don't mind ghosts when there's two of us. Besides which, the noise of the pistol 'll wake up 'arf the river."

"You take care you don't get woke up," ses Joe, 'ardly able to speak for temper.

He went off stamping, and grinding 'is teeth, and at eight o'clock to the minute, Ted Dennis turned up with 'is pistol and helped me take care of the wharf. Happy as a skylark 'e was, and to see him 'iding behind a barrel with his pistol ready, waiting for the ghost, a'most made me forget the expense of it all.

It never came near us that night, and Ted was a bit disappointed next morning as he took 'is ninepence and went off. Next night was the same, and the next, and then Ted gave up hiding on the wharf for it, and sat and snoozed in the office instead.

A week went by, and then another, and still there was no sign of Sam Bullet's ghost, or Joe Peel, and every morning I 'ad to try and work up a smile as I shelled out ninepence for Ted. It nearly ruined me, and, worse than that, I couldn't explain why I was short to the missis. Fust of all she asked me wot I was spending it on, then she asked me who I was spending it on. It nearly broke up my 'ome— she did smash one kitchen-chair and a vase off the parlour mantelpiece—but I wouldn't tell 'er, and then, led away by some men on strike at Smith's wharf, Ted went on strike for a bob a night.

That was arter he 'ad been with me for three weeks, and when Saturday came, of course I was more short than ever, and people came and stood at their doors all the way down our street to listen to the missis taking my character away.

I stood it as long as I could, and then, when 'er back was turned for 'arf a moment, I slipped out. While she'd been talking I'd been thinking, and it came to me clear as daylight that there was no need for me to sacrifice myself any longer looking arter a dead man's watch and chain.

I didn't know exactly where Joe Peel lived, but I knew the part, and arter peeping into seven public-'ouses I see the man I wanted sitting by 'imself in a little bar. I walked in quiet-like, and sat down opposite 'im.

"Morning," I ses.

Joe Peel grunted.

"'Ave one with me?" I ses.

He grunted agin, but not quite so fierce, and I fetched the two pints from the counter and took a seat alongside of 'im.

"I've been looking for you," I ses.

"Oh!" he ses, looking me up and down and all over. "Well, you've found me now."

"I want to talk to you about the ghost of pore Sam Bullet," I ses.

Joe Peel put 'is mug down sudden and looked at me fierce. "Look 'ere! Don't you come and try to be funny with me," he ses. "'Cos I won't 'ave it."

"I don't want to be funny," I ses. "Wot I want to know is, are you in the same mind about that watch and chain as you was the other day?"

He didn't seem to be able to speak at fust, but arter a time 'e gives a gasp. "Woes the game?" he ses.

"Wot I want to know is, if I give you that watch and chain for fifteen bob, will that keep the ghost from 'anging round my wharf agin?" I ses.

"Why, o' course," he ses, staring; "but you ain't been seeing it agin, 'ave you?"

"I've not, and I don't want to," I ses. "If it wants you to 'ave the watch and chain, give me the fifteen bob, and it's yours."

He looked at me for a moment as if he couldn't believe 'is eyesight, and then 'e puts his 'and into 'is trowsis-pocket and pulls out one shilling and fourpence, 'arf a clay-pipe, and a bit o' lead-pencil.

"That's all I've got with me," he ses. "I'll owe you the rest. You ought to ha' took the fifteen bob when I 'ad it."

There was no 'elp for it, and arter making 'im swear to give me the rest o' the money when 'e got it, and that I shouldn't see the ghost agin, I 'anded the things over to 'im and came away. He came to the door to see me off, and if ever a man looked puzzled, 'e did. Pleased at the same time.

It was a load off of my mind. My con-science told me I'd done right, and arter sending a little boy with a note to Ted Dennis to tell 'im not to come any more, I felt 'appier than I 'ad done for a long time. When I got to the wharf that evening it seemed like a diff'rent place, and I was whistling and smiling over my work quite in my old way, when the young policeman passed.

"Hullo !" he ses. "'Ave you seen the ghost agin?"

"I 'ave not," I ses, drawing myself up. "'Ave you?"

"No," he ses.

"We missed it."

"Missed it?" I ses, staring at 'im.

"Yes," he ses, nodding. "The day arter you came out screaming, and cuddling me like a frightened baby, it shipped as A.B. on the barque Ocean King, for Valparaiso. We missed it by a few hours. Next time you see a ghost, knock it down fust and go and cuddle the police arterwards."

SELF-HELP

The night-watchman sat brooding darkly over life and its troubles. A shooting corn on the little toe of his left foot, and a touch of liver, due, he was convinced, to the unlawful cellar work of the landlord of the Queen's Head, had induced in him a vein of profound depression. A discarded boot stood by his side, and his gray-stockinged foot protruded over the edge of the jetty until a passing waterman gave it a playful rap with his oar. A subsequent inquiry as to the price of pigs' trotters fell on ears rendered deaf by suffering.

"I might 'ave expected it," said the watchman, at last. "I done that man—if you can call him a man—a kindness once, and this is my reward for it. Do a man a kindness, and years arterwards 'e comes along and hits you over your tenderest corn with a oar."

He took up his boot, and, inserting his foot with loving care, stooped down and fastened the laces.

Do a man a kindness, he continued, assuming a safer posture, and 'e tries to borrow money off of you; do a woman a kindness and she thinks you want tr marry 'er; do an animal a kindness and it tries to bite you—same as a horse bit a sailorman I knew once, when 'e sat on its head to 'elp it get up. He sat too far for'ard, pore chap.

Kindness never gets any thanks. I remember a man whose pal broke 'is leg while they was working together unloading a barge; and he went off to break the news to 'is pal's wife. A kind-'earted man 'e was as ever you see, and, knowing 'ow she would take on when she 'eard the news, he told her fust of all that 'er husband was killed. She took on like a mad thing, and at last, when she couldn't do anything more and 'ad quieted down a bit, he told 'er that it was on'y a case of a broken leg, thinking that 'er joy would be so great that she wouldn't think anything of that. He 'ad to tell her three times afore she understood 'im, and then, instead of being thankful to 'im for 'is thoughtfulness, she chased him 'arf over Wapping with a chopper, screaming with temper.

I remember Ginger Dick and Peter Russet trying to do old Sam Small a kindness one time when they was 'aving a rest ashore arter a v'y'ge. They 'ad took a room together as usual, and for the fust two or three days they was like brothers. That couldn't last, o' course, and Sam was so annoyed one evening at Ginger's suspiciousness by biting a 'arf-dollar Sam owed 'im and finding it was a bad 'un, that 'e went off to spend the evening all alone by himself.

He felt a bit dull at fust, but arter he had 'ad two or three 'arf-pints 'e began to take a brighter view of things. He found a very nice, cosey little public-'ouse he hadn't been in before, and, arter getting two and threepence and a pint for the 'arf-dollar with Ginger's tooth-marks on, he began to think that the world wasn't 'arf as bad a place as people tried to make out.

There was on'y one other man in the little bar Sam was in—a tall, dark chap, with black side-whiskers and spectacles, wot kept peeping round the partition and looking very 'ard at everybody that came in.

"I'm just keeping my eye on 'em, cap'n," he ses to Sam, in a low voice.

"Ho!" ses Sam.

"They don't know me in this disguise," ses the dark man, "but I see as 'ow you spotted me at once. Anybody 'ud have a 'ard time of it to deceive you; and then they wouldn't gain nothing by it."

"Nobody ever 'as yet," ses Sam, smiling at 'im.

"And nobody ever will," ses the dark man, shaking his 'ead; "if they was all as fly as you, I might as well put the shutters up. How did you twig I was a detective officer, cap'n?"

Sam, wot was taking a drink, got some beer up 'is nose with surprise.

"That's my secret," he ses, arter the tec 'ad patted 'im on the back and brought 'im round.

"You're a marvel, that's wot you are," ses the tec, shaking his 'ead. "Have one with me."

Sam said he didn't mind if 'e did, and arter drinking each other's healths very perlite 'e ordered a couple o' twopenny smokes, and by way of showing off paid for 'em with 'arf a quid.

"That's right, ain't it?" ses the barmaid, as he stood staring very 'ard at the change. "I ain't sure about that 'arf-crown, now I come to look at it; but it's the one you gave me."

Pore Sam, with a tec standing alongside of 'im, said it was quite right, and put it into 'is pocket in a hurry and began to talk to the tec as fast as he could about a murder he 'ad been reading about in the paper that morning. They went and sat down by a comfortable little fire that was burning in the bar, and the tec told 'im about a lot o' murder cases he 'ad been on himself.

"I'm down 'ere now on special work," he ses, "looking arter sailormen."

"Wot ha' they been doing?" ses Sam.

"When I say looking arter, I mean protecting 'em," ses the tec. "Over and over agin some pore feller, arter working 'ard for months at sea, comes 'ome with a few pounds in 'is pocket and gets robbed of the lot. There's a couple o' chaps down 'ere I'm told off to look arter special, but it's no good unless I can catch 'em red-'anded."

"Red-'anded?" ses Sam.

"With their hands in the chap's pockets, I mean," ses the tec.

Sam gave a shiver. "Somebody had their 'ands in my pockets once," he ses. "Four pun ten and some coppers they got."

"Wot was they like?" ses the tee, starting.

Sam shook his 'ead. "They seemed to me to be all hands, that's all I know about 'em," he ses. "Arter they 'ad finished they leaned me up agin the dock wall an' went off."

"It sounds like 'em," ses the tec, thoughtfully. "It was Long Pete and Fair Alf, for a quid; that's the two I'm arter."

He put his finger in 'is weskit-pocket. "That's who I am," he ses, 'anding Sam a card; "Detective-Sergeant Cubbins. If you ever get into any trouble at any time, you come to me."

Sam said 'e would, and arter they had 'ad another drink together the tec shifted 'is seat alongside of 'im and talked in his ear.

"If I can nab them two chaps I shall get promotion," he ses; "and it's a fi'-pun note to anybody that helps me. I wish I could persuade you to."

"'Ow's it to be done?" ses Sam, looking at 'im.

"I want a respectable-looking seafaring man," ses the tec, speaking very slow; "that's you. He goes up Tower Hill to-morrow night at nine o'clock, walking very slow and very unsteady on 'is pins, and giving my two beauties the idea that 'e is three sheets in the wind. They come up and rob 'im, and I catch them red-'anded. I get promotion, and you get a fiver."

"But 'ow do you know they'll be there?" ses Sam, staring at 'im.

Mr. Cubbins winked at 'im and tapped 'is nose.

"We 'ave to know a good deal in our line o' business," he ses.

"Still," ses Sam, "I don't see—"

"Narks," says the tec; "coppers' narks. You've 'eard of them, cap'n? Now, look 'ere. Have you got any money?"

"I got a matter o' twelve quid or so," ses Sam, in a of hand way.

"The very thing," says the tec. "Well, to-morrow night you put that in your pocket, and be walking up Tower Hill just as the clock strikes nine. I promise you you'll be robbed afore two minutes past, and by two and a 'arf past I shall 'ave my hands on both of 'em. Have all the money in one pocket, so as they can get it neat and quick, in case they get interrupted. Better still, 'ave it in a purse; that makes it easier to bring it 'ome to 'em."

"Wouldn't it be enough if they stole the purse?" ses Sam. "I should feel safer that way, too."

Mr. Cubbins shook his 'ead, very slow and solemn. "That wouldn't do at all," he ses. "The more money they steal, the longer they'll get; you know that, cap'n, without me telling you. If you could put fifty quid in it would be so much the better. And, what-ever you do, don't make a noise. I don't want a lot o' clumsy policemen interfering in my business."

"Still, s'pose you didn't catch 'em," ses Sam, "where should I be?"

"You needn't be afraid o' that," ses the tec, with a laugh. "Here, I'll tell you wot I'll do, and that'll show you the trust I put in you."

He drew a big di'mond ring off of 'is finger and handed it to Sam.

"Put that on your finger," he ses, "and keep it there till I give you your money back and the fi'-pun note reward. It's worth seventy quid if it's worth a farthing, and was given to me by a lady of title for getting back 'er jewellery for 'er. Put it on, and wotever you do, don't lose it"

He sat and watched while Sam forced it on is finger.

"You don't need to flash it about too much," he ses, looking at 'im rather anxious. "There's men I know as 'ud cut your finger off to get that."

Sam shoved his 'and in his pocket, but he kept taking it out every now and then and 'olding his finger up to the light to look at the di'mond. Mr. Cubbins got up to go at last, saying that he 'ad got a call to make at the police-station, and they went out together.

"Nine o'clock sharp," he ses, as they shook hands, "on Tower Hill."

"I'll be there," ses Sam.

"And, wotever you do, no noise, no calling out," ses the tec, "and don't mention a word of this to a living soul."

Sam shook 'ands with 'im agin, and then, hiding his 'and in his pocket, went off 'ome, and, finding Ginger and Peter Russet wasn't back, went off to bed.

He 'eard 'em coming upstairs in the dark in about an hour's time, and, putting the 'and with the ring on it on the counterpane, shut 'is eyes and pretended to be fast asleep. Ginger lit the candle, and they was both beginning to undress when Peter made a noise and pointed to Sam's 'and.

"Wot's up?" ses Ginger, taking the candle and going over to Sam's bed. "Who've you been robbing, you fat pirate?"

Sam kept 'is eyes shut and 'eard 'em whispering; then he felt 'em take 'is hand up and look at it. "Where did you get it, Sam?" ses Peter.

"He's asleep," ses Ginger, "sound asleep. I b'lieve if I was to put 'is finger in the candle he wouldn't wake up."

"You try it," ses Sam, sitting up in bed very sharp and snatching his 'and away. "Wot d'ye mean coming 'ome at all hours and waking me up?" "Where did you get that ring?" ses Ginger. "Friend o' mine," ses Sam, very short.

"Who was it?" ses Peter.

"It's a secret," ses Sam.

"You wouldn't 'ave a secret from your old pal Ginger, Sam, would you?" ses Ginger.

"Old wot?" ses Sam. "Wot did you call me this arternoon?"

"I called you a lot o' things I'm sorry for," ses Ginger, who was bursting with curiosity, "and I beg your pardin, Sam."

"Shake 'ands on it," ses Peter, who was nearly as curious as Ginger.

They shook hands, but Sam said he couldn't tell 'em about the ring; and several times Ginger was on the point of calling 'im the names he 'ad called 'im in the arternoon, on'y Peter trod on 'is foot and stopped him. They wouldn't let 'im go to sleep for talking, and at last, when 'e was pretty near tired out, he told 'em all about it.

"Going—to 'ave your—pocket picked?" ses Ginger, staring at 'im, when 'e had finished.

"I shall be watched over," ses Sam.

"He's gorn stark, staring mad," ses Ginger. "Wot a good job it is he's got me and you to look arter 'im, Peter."

"Wot d'ye mean?" ses Sam.

"*Mean?*" ses Ginger. "Why, it's a put-up job to rob you, o' course. I should ha' thought even your fat 'ead could ha' seen that':"

"When I want your advice I'll ask you for it," ses Sam, losing 'is temper. "Wot about the di'mond ring—eh?"

"You stick to it," ses Ginger, "and keep out o' Mr. Cubbins's way. That's my advice to you. 'Sides, p'r'aps it ain't a real one."

Sam told 'im agin he didn't want none of 'is advice, and, as Ginger wouldn't leave off talking, he pretended to go to sleep. Ginger woke 'im up three times to tell 'im wot a fool 'e was, but 'e got so fierce that he gave it up at last and told 'im to go 'is own way.

Sam wouldn't speak to either of 'em next morning, and arter breakfast he went off on 'is own. He came back while Peter and Ginger was out, and they wasted best part o' the day trying to find 'im.

"We'll be on Tower Hill just afore nine and keep 'im out o' mischief, any way," ses Peter.

Ginger nodded. "And be called names for our pains," he ses. "I've a good mind to let 'im be robbed."

"It 'ud serve 'im right," ses Peter, "on'y then he'd want to borrer off of us. Look here! Why not—why not rob 'im ourselves?"

"Wot?" ses Ginger, starting.

"Walk up behind 'im and rob 'im," ses Peter. "He'll think it's them two chaps he spoke about, and when 'e comes 'ome complaining to us we'll tell 'im it serves 'im right. Arter we've 'ad a game with 'im for a day or two we'll give 'im 'is money back."

"But he'd reckernize us," ses Ginger.

"We must disguise ourselves," ses Peter, in a whisper. "There's a barber's shop in Cable Street, where I've seen beards in the winder. You hook 'em on over your ears. Get one o' them each, pull our caps over our eyes and turn our collars up, and there you are."

Ginger made a lot of objections, not because he didn't think it was a good idea, but because he didn't like Peter thinking of it instead of 'im; but he gave way at last, and, arter he 'ad got the beard, he stood for a long time in front o' the glass thinking wot a difference it would ha' made to his looks if he had 'ad black 'air instead o' red.

Waiting for the evening made the day seem very long to 'em; but it came at last, and, with the beards in their pockets, they slipped out and went for a walk round. They 'ad 'arf a pint each at a public-'ouse at the top of the Minories, just to steady themselves, and then they came out and hooked on their beards; and wot with them, and pulling their caps down and turning their coat-collars up, there wasn't much of their faces to be seen by anybody.

It was just five minutes to nine when they got to Tower Hill, and they walked down the middle of the road, keeping a bright lookout for old Sam. A little way down they saw a couple o' chaps leaning up agin a closed gate in the dock wall lighting their pipes, and Peter and Ginger both nudged each other with their elbows at the same time. They 'ad just got to the bottom of the Hill when Sam turned the corner.

Peter wouldn't believe at fust that the old man wasn't really the worse for liquor, 'e was so lifelike. Many a drunken man would ha' been proud to ha' done it 'arf so well, and it made 'im pleased to think that Sam was a pal of 'is. Him and Ginger turned and crept up behind the old man on tiptoe, and then all of a sudden he tilted Sam's cap over 'is eyes and flung his arms round 'im, while Ginger felt in 'is coat-pockets and took out a leather purse chock full o' money.

It was all done and over in a moment, and then, to Ginger's great surprise, Sam suddenly lifted 'is foot and gave 'im a fearful kick on the shin of 'is leg, and at the same time let drive with all his might in 'is face. Ginger went down as if he 'ad been shot, and as Peter went to 'elp him up he got a bang over the 'ead that put 'im alongside o' Ginger, arter which Sam turned and trotted off down the Hill like a dancing-bear.

For 'arf a minute Ginger didn't know where 'e was, and afore he found out the two men they'd seen in the gateway came up, and one of 'em put his knee in Ginger's back and 'eld him, while the other caught hold of his 'and and dragged the purse out of it. Arter which they both made off up the Hill as 'ard as they could go, while Peter Russet in a faint voice called "Police!" arter them.

He got up presently and helped Ginger up, and they both stood there pitying themselves, and 'elping each other to think of names to call Sam.

"Well, the money's gorn, and it's 'is own silly fault," ses Ginger. "But wotever 'appens, he mustn't know that we had a 'and in it, mind that."

"He can starve for all I care," ses Peter, feeling his 'ead. "I won't lend 'im a ha'penny—not a single, blessed ha'penny."

"Who'd ha' thought 'e could ha' hit like that?" says Ginger. "That's wot gets over me. I never 'ad such a bang in my life—never. I'm going to 'ave a little drop o' brandy—my 'ead is fair swimming."

Peter 'ad one, too; but though they went into the private bar, it wasn't private enough for them; and when the landlady asked Ginger who'd been kissing 'im, he put 'is glass down with a bang and walked straight off 'ome.

Sam 'adn't turned up by the time they got there, and pore Ginger took advantage of it to put a little warm candle-grease on 'is bad leg. Then he bathed 'is face very careful and 'elped Peter bathe his 'ead. They 'ad just finished when they heard Sam coming upstairs, and Ginger sat down on 'is bed and began to whistle, while Peter took up a bit o' newspaper and stood by the candle reading it.

"Lor' lumme, Ginger!" ses Sam, staring at 'im. "What ha' you been a-doing to your face?"

"Me?" ses Ginger, careless-like. "Oh, we 'ad a bit of a scrap down Limehouse way with some Scotchies. Peter got a crack over the 'ead at the same time."

"Ah, I've 'ad a bit of a scrap, too," ses Sam, smiling all over, "but I didn't get marked."

"Oh!" ses Peter, without looking up from 'is paper. "Was it a little boy, then?" ses Ginger.

"No, it wasn't a little boy neither, Ginger," ses Sam; "it was a couple o' men twice the size of you and Peter here, and I licked 'em both. It was the two men I spoke to you about last night."

"Oh!" ses Peter agin, yawning.

"I did a bit o' thinking this morning," ses Sam, nodding at 'em, "and I don't mind owning up that it was owing to wot you said. You was right, Ginger, arter all."

"Fust thing I did arter breakfast," ses Sam, "I took that di'mond ring to a pawnshop and found out it wasn't a di'mond ring. Then I did a bit more thinking, and I went round to a shop I know and bought a couple o' knuckle-dusters."

"Couple o' wot?" ses Ginger, in a choking voice.

"Knuckle-dusters," ses Sam, "and I turned up to-night at Tower Hill with one on each 'and just as the clock was striking nine. I see 'em the moment I turned the corner—two enormous big chaps, a yard acrost the shoulders, coming down the middle of the road—You've got a cold, Ginger!"

"No, I ain't," ses Ginger.

"I pretended to be drunk, same as the tec told me," ses Sam, "and then I felt 'em turn round and creep up behind me. One of 'em come up behind and put 'is knee in my back and caught me by the throat, and the other gave me a punch in the chest, and while I was gasping for breath took my purse away. Then I started on 'em."

"Lor'!" ses Ginger, very nasty.

"I fought like a lion," ses Sam. "Twice they 'ad me down, and twice I got up agin and hammered 'em. They both of 'em 'ad knives, but my blood was up, and I didn't take no more notice of 'em than if they was made of paper. I knocked 'em both out o' their hands, and if I hit 'em in the face once I did a dozen times. I surprised myself."

"You surprise me," ses Ginger.

"All of a sudden," ses Sam, "they see they 'ad got to do with a man wot didn't know wot fear was, and they turned round and ran off as hard as they could run. You ought to ha' been there, Ginger. You'd 'ave enjoyed it."

Ginger Dick didn't answer 'im. Having to sit still and listen to all them lies without being able to say anything nearly choked 'im. He sat there gasping for breath.

"O' course, you got your purse back in the fight, Sam?" ses Peter.

"No, mate," ses Sam. "I ain't going to tell you no lies—I did not."

"And 'ow are you going to live, then, till you get a ship, Sam?" ses Ginger, in a nasty voice. "You won't get nothing out o' me, so you needn't think it."

"Wot on earth's the matter, Ginger?"

"Nor me," ses Peter. "Not a brass farthing."

"There's no call to be nasty about it, mates," ses Sam. "I 'ad the best fight I ever 'ad in my life, and I must put up with the loss. A man can't 'ave it all his own way."

"'Ow much was it?" ses Peter.

"Ten brace-buttons, three French ha'pennies, and a bit o' tin," ses Sam. "Wot on earth's the matter, Ginger?"

Ginger didn't answer him.

SENTENCE DEFERRED

Fortunately for Captain Bligh, there were but few people about, and the only person who saw him trip Police-Sergeant Pilbeam was an elderly man with a wooden leg, who joined the indignant officer in the pursuit. The captain had youth on his side, and, diving into the narrow alley-ways that constitute the older portion of Wood-hatch, he moderated his pace and listened acutely. The sounds of pursuit died away in the distance, and he had already dropped into a walk when the hurried tap of the wooden leg sounded from one corner and a chorus of hurried voices from the other. It was clear that the number of hunters had increased.

He paused a second, irresolute. The next, he pushed open a door that stood ajar in an old flint wall and peeped in. He saw a small, brick-paved yard, in which trim myrtles and flowering plants stood about in freshly ochred pots, and, opening the door a little wider, he slipped in and closed it behind him.

"Well?" said a voice, sharply. "What do you want?"

Captain Bligh turned, and saw a girl standing in a hostile attitude in the doorway of the house. "H'sh!" he said, holding up his finger.

The girl's cheeks flushed and her eyes sparkled.

"What are you doing in our yard?" she demanded.

The captain's face relaxed as the sound of voices died away. He gave his moustache a twist, and eyed her with frank admiration.

"Escaping," he said, briefly. "They nearly had me, though."

"You had no business to escape into our yard," said the girl. "What have you been escaping from?"

"Fat policeman," said the skipper, jauntily, twisting his moustache.

Miss Pilbeam, only daughter of Sergeant Pilbeam, caught her breath sharply.

"What have you been doing?" she inquired, as soon as she could control her voice.

"Nothing," said the skipper, airily, "nothing. I was kicking a stone along the path and he told me to stop it."

"Well?" said Miss Pilbeam, impatiently.

"We had words," said the skipper. "I don't like policemen—fat policemen—and while we were talking he happened to lose his balance and go over into some mud that was swept up at the side of the road."

"Lost his balance?" gasped the horrified Miss Pilbeam.

The skipper was flattered at her concern. "You would have laughed if you had seen him," he said, smiling. "Don't look so frightened; he hasn't got me yet."

"No," said the girl, slowly. "Not yet."

She gazed at him with such a world of longing in her eyes that the skipper, despite a somewhat large share of self-esteem, was almost startled.

"And he shan't have me," he said, returning her gaze with interest.

Miss Pilbeam stood in silent thought. She was a strong, well-grown girl, but she realized fully that she was no match for the villain who stood before her, twisting his moustache and adjusting his neck-tie. And her father would not be off duty until nine.

"I suppose you would like to wait here until it is dark?" she said at last.

"I would sooner wait here than anywhere," said the skipper, with respectful ardor.

"Perhaps you would like to come in and sit down?" said the girl.

Captain Bligh thanked her, and removing his cap followed her into a small parlor in the front of the house.

"Father is out," she said, as she motioned him to an easy-chair, "but I'm sure he'll be pleased to see you when he comes in."

"And I shall be pleased to see him," said the innocent skipper.

Miss Pilbeam kept her doubts to herself and sat in a brown study, wondering how the capture was to be effected. She had a strong presentiment that the appearance of her father at the front door would be the signal for her visitor's departure at the back. For a time there was an awkward silence.

"Lucky thing for me I upset that policeman," said the skipper, at last.

"Why?" inquired the girl.

"Else I shouldn't have come into your yard," was the reply. "It's the first time we have ever put into Woodhatch, and I might have sailed away and never seen you. Where should we have been but for that fat policeman?"

Miss Pilbeam—as soon as she could get her breath—said, "Ah, where indeed!" and for the first time in her life began to feel the need of a chaperon.

"Funny to think of him hunting for me high and low while I am sitting here," said the skipper.

Miss Pilbeam agreed with him, and began to laugh—to laugh so heartily that he was fain at last to draw his chair close to hers and pat her somewhat anxiously on the back. The treatment sobered her at once, and she drew apart and eyed him coldly.

"I was afraid you would lose your breath," explained the skipper, awkwardly. "You are not angry, are you?"

He was so genuinely relieved when she said, "No," that Miss Pilbeam, despite her father's wrongs, began to soften a little. The upsetter of policemen was certainly good-looking; and his manner towards her so nicely balanced between boldness and timidity that a slight feeling of sadness at his lack of moral character began to assail her.

"Suppose you are caught after all?" she said, presently. "You will go to prison."

The skipper shrugged his shoulders. "I don't suppose I shall be," he replied.

"Aren't you sorry?" persisted Miss Pilbeam, in a vibrant voice.

"Certainly not," said the skipper. "Why, I shouldn't have seen you if I hadn't done it."

Miss Pilbeam looked at the clock and pondered. It wanted but five minutes to nine. Five minutes in which to make up a mind that was in a state of strong unrest.

"I suppose it is time for me to go," said the skipper, watching her. Miss Pilbeam rose. "No, don't go," she said, hastily. "Do be quiet. I want to think."

Captain Bligh waited in respectful silence, heedless of the fateful seconds ticking from the mantelpiece. At the sound of a slow, measured footfall on the cobblestone path outside Miss Pilbeam caught his arm and drew him towards the door.

"Go!" she breathed. "No, stop!"

She stood trying in vain to make up her mind. "Upstairs," she said. "Quick!" and, leading the way, entered her father's bedroom, and, after a moment's thought, opened the door of a cupboard in the corner.

"Get in there," she whispered.

"But—" objected the astonished Bligh.

The front door was heard to open.

"Police!" said Miss Pilbeam, in a thrilling whisper. The skipper stepped into the cupboard without further parley, and the girl, turning the key, slipped it into her pocket and sped downstairs.

Sergeant Pilbeam was in the easy-chair, with his belt unfastened, when she entered the parlor, and, with a hungry reference to supper, sat watching her as she lit the lamp and drew down the blind. With a lifelong knowledge of the requirements of the Force, she drew a jug of beer and placed it by his side while she set the table.

"Ah! I wanted that," said the sergeant. "I've been running."

Miss Pilbeam raised her eyebrows.

"After some sailor-looking chap that capsized me when I wasn't prepared for it," said her father, putting down his glass. "It was a neat bit o' work, and I shall tell him so when I catch him. Look here!"

He stood up and exhibited the damage.

"I've rubbed off what I could," he said, resuming his seat, "and I s'pose the rest'll brush off when it's dry. To-morrow morning I shall go down to the harbor and try and spot my lord."

He drew his chair to the table and helped himself, and, filling his mouth with cold meat and pickles, enlarged on his plans for the capture of his assailant; plans to which the undecided Miss Pilbeam turned a somewhat abstracted ear.

By the time her father had finished his supper she was trying, but in vain, to devise means for the prisoner's escape. The sergeant had opened the door of the room for the sake of fresh air, and it was impossible for anybody to come downstairs without being seen. The story of a sickly geranium in the back-yard left him unmoved.

"I wouldn't get up for all the geraniums in the world," he declared. "I'm just going to have one more pipe and then I'm off to bed. Running don't agree with me."

He went, despite his daughter's utmost efforts to prevent him, and she sat in silent consternation, listening to his heavy tread overhead. She heard the bed creak in noisy protest as he climbed in, and ten minutes later the lusty snoring of a healthy man of full habit resounded through the house.

She went to bed herself at last, and, after lying awake for nearly a couple of hours, closed her eyes in order to think better. She awoke with the sun pouring in at the window and the sounds of vigorous brushing in the yard beneath.

"I've nearly got it off," said the sergeant, looking up. "It's destroying evidence in a sense, I suppose; but I can't go about with my uniform plastered with mud. I've had enough chaff about it as it is."

Miss Pilbeam stole to the door of the next room and peeped stealthily in. Not a sound came from the cupboard, and a horrible idea that the prisoner might have been suffocated set her trembling with apprehension.

"H'sh!" she whispered.

An eager but stifled "H'st!" came from the cup-board, and Miss Pilbeam, her fears allayed, stepped softly into the room.

"He's downstairs brushing the mud off," she said, in a low voice.

"Who is?" said the skipper.

"The fat policeman," said the girl, in a hard voice, as she remembered her father's wrongs.

"What's he doing it here for?" demanded the astonished skipper.

"Because he lives here."

"Lodger?" queried the skipper, more astonished than before.

"Father," said Miss Pilbeam.

A horrified groan from the cupboard fell like music on her ears. Then the smile forsook her lips, and she stood quivering with indignation as the groan gave way to suppressed but unmistakable laughter.

"H'sh!" she said sharply, and with head erect sailed out of the room and went downstairs to give Mr. Pilbeam his breakfast.

To the skipper in the confined space and darkness of the cupboard the breakfast seemed unending. The sergeant evidently believed in sitting over his meals, and his deep, rumbling voice, punctuated by good-natured laughter, was plainly audible. To pass the time the skipper fell to counting, and, tired of that, recited some verses that he had acquired at school. After that, and with far more heartiness, he declaimed a few things that he had learned since; and still the clatter and rumble sounded from below.

It was a relief to him when he heard the sergeant push his chair back and move heavily about the room. A minute later he heard him ascending the stairs, and then he held his breath with horror as the foot-steps entered the room and a heavy hand was laid on the cupboard door.

"Elsie!" bawled the sergeant. "Where's the key of my cupboard? I want my other boots."

"They're down here," cried the voice of Miss Pilbeam, and the skipper, hardly able to believe in his good fortune, heard the sergeant go downstairs again.

At the expiration of another week—by his own reckoning—he heard the light, hurried footsteps of Miss Pilbeam come up the stairs and pause at the door.

"H'st!" he said, recklessly.

"I'm coming," said the girl. "Don't be impatient."

A key turned in the lock, the door was flung open, and the skipper, dazed and blinking with the sudden light, stumbled into the room.

"Father's gone," said Miss Pilbeam.

The skipper made no answer. He was administering first aid to a right leg which had temporarily forgotten how to perform its duties, varied with slaps and pinches at a left which had gone to sleep. At intervals he turned a red-rimmed and reproachful eye on Miss Pilbeam.

"You want a wash and some breakfast," she said, softly, "especially a wash. There's water and a towel, and while you're making yourself tidy I'll be getting breakfast."

The skipper hobbled to the wash-stand, and, dipping his head in a basin of cool water, began to feel himself again. By the time he had done his hair in the sergeant's glass and twisted his moustache into shape he felt better still, and he went downstairs almost blithely.

"I'm very sorry it was your father," he said, as he took a seat at the table. "Very."

"That's why you laughed, I suppose?" said the girl, tossing her head.

"Well, I've had the worst of it," said the other. "I'd sooner be upset a hundred times than spend a night in that cupboard. However, all's well that ends well."

"Ah!" said Miss Pilbeam, dolefully, "but is it the end?"

Captain Bligh put down his knife and fork and eyed her uneasily.

"What do you mean?" he said.

"Never mind; don't spoil your breakfast," said the girl. "I'll tell you afterwards. It's horrid to think, after all my trouble, of your doing two months as well as a night in the cupboard."

"Beastly," said the unfortunate, eying her in great concern. "But what's the matter?"

"One can't think of everything," said Miss Pilbeam, "but, of course, we ought to have thought of the mate getting uneasy when you didn't turn up last night, and going to the police-station with a description of you."

The skipper started and smote the table with his fist.

"Father's gone down to watch the ship now," said Miss Pilbeam. "Of course, it's the exact description of the man that assaulted him. Providential he called it."

"That's the worst of having a fool for a mate," said the skipper, bitterly. "What business was it of his, I should like to know? What's it got to do with him whether I turn up or not? What does he want to interfere for?"

"It's no good blaming him," said Miss Pilbeam, thinking deeply, with her chin on her finger. "The thing is, what is to be done? Once father gets his hand on you—"

She shuddered; so did the skipper.

"I might get off with a fine; I didn't hurt him," he remarked.

Miss Pilbeam shook her head. "They're very strict in Woodhatch," she said.

"I was a fool to touch him at all," said the repentant skipper. "High spirits, that's what it was. High spirits, and being spoken to as if I was a child."

"The thing is, how are you to escape?" said the girl. "It's no good going out of doors with the police and half the people in Woodhatch all on the look-out for you."

"If I could only get aboard I should be all right," muttered the skipper. "I could keep down the fo'-c's'le while the mate took the ship out."

Miss Pilbeam sat in deep thought. "It's the getting aboard that's the trouble," she said, slowly. "You'd have to disguise yourself. It would have to be a good disguise, too, to pass my father, I can tell you."

Captain Bligh gave a gloomy assent.

"The only thing for you to do, so far as I can see," said the girl, slowly, "is to make yourself up like a coalie. There are one or two colliers in the harbor, and if you took off your coat—I could send it on afterwards—rubbed yourself all over with coal-dust, and shaved off your moustache, I believe you would escape."

"Shave!" ejaculated the skipper, in choking accents. "Rub—! Coal-dust!"

"It's your only chance," said Miss Pilbeam.

Captain Bligh leaned back frowning, and from sheer force of habit passed the ends of his moustache slowly through his fingers. "I think the coal-dust would be enough," he said at last.

The girl shook her head. "Father particularly noticed your moustache," she said.

"Everybody does," said the skipper, with mournful pride. "I won't part with it."

"Not for my sake?" inquired Miss Pilbeam, eying him mournfully. "Not after all I've done for you?"

"No," said the other, stoutly.

Miss Pilbeam put her handkerchief to her eyes and, with a suspicious little sniff, hurried from the room. Captain Bligh, much affected, waited for a few seconds and then went in pursuit of her. Fifteen minutes later, shorn of his moustache, he stood in the coal-hole, sulkily smearing himself with coal.

"That's better," said the girl; "you look horrible."

She took up a handful of coal-dust and, ordering him to stoop, shampooed him with hearty good-will.

"No good half doing it," she declared. "Now go and look at yourself in the glass in the kitchen."

The skipper went, and came back in a state of wild-eyed misery. Even Miss Pilbeam's statement that his own mother would not know him failed to lift the cloud from his brow. He stood disconsolate as the girl opened the front door.

"Good-by," she said, gently. "Write and tell me when you are safe."

Captain Bligh promised, and walked slowly up the road. So far from people attempting to arrest him, they vied with each other in giving him elbow-room. He reached the harbor unmolested, and, lurking at a convenient corner, made a careful survey. A couple of craft were working out their coal, a small steamer was just casting loose, and a fishing-boat gliding slowly over the still water to its berth. His own schooner, which lay near the colliers, had apparently knocked off work pending his arrival. For Sergeant Pilbeam he looked in vain.

He waited a minute or two, and then, with a furtive glance right and left, strolled in a careless fashion until he was abreast of one of the colliers. Nobody took any notice of him, and, with his hands in his pockets, he gazed meditatively into the water and edged along towards his own craft. His foot trembled as he placed it on the plank that formed the gangway, but, resisting the temptation to look behind, he gained the deck and walked forward.

"Halloa! What do you want?" inquired a sea-man, coming out of the galley.

"All right, Bill," said the skipper, in a low voice. "Don't take any notice of me."

"Eh?" said the seaman, starting. "Good lor'! What ha' you—"

"Shut up!" said the skipper, fiercely; and, walking to the forecastle, placed his hand on the scuttle and descended with studied slowness. As he reached the floor the perturbed face of Bill blocked the opening.

"Had an accident, cap'n?" he inquired, respectfully.

"No," snapped the skipper. "Come down here—quick! Don't stand up there attracting attention. Do you want the whole town round you? Come down!"

"I'm all right where I am," said Bill, backing hastily as the skipper, putting a foot on the ladder, thrust a black and furious face close to his.

"Clear out, then," hissed the skipper. "Go and send the mate to me. Don't hurry. And if anybody noticed me come aboard and should ask you who I am, say I'm a pal of yours."

The seaman, marvelling greatly, withdrew, and the skipper, throwing himself on a locker, wiped a bit of grit out of his eye and sat down to wait for the mate. He was so long in coming that he waxed impatient, and ascending a step of the ladder again peeped on to the deck. The first object that met his gaze was the figure of the mate leaning against the side of the ship with a wary eye on the scuttle.

"Come here," said the skipper.

"Anything wrong?" inquired the mate, retreating a couple of paces in disorder.

"Come—here!" repeated the skipper.

The mate advanced slowly, and in response to an imperative command from the skipper slowly descended and stood regarding him nervously.

"Yes; you may look," said the skipper, with sudden ferocity. "This is all your doing. Where are you going?"

He caught the mate by the coat as he was making for the ladder, and hauled him back again.

"You'll go when I've finished with you," he said, grimly. "Now, what do you mean by it? Eh? What do you mean by it?"

"That's all right," said the mate, in a soothing voice. "Don't get excited."

"Look at me!" said the skipper. "All through your interfering. How dare you go making inquiries about me?"

"Me?" said the mate, backing as far as possible. "Inquiries?"

"What's it got to do with you if I stay out all night?" pursued the skipper.

"Nothing," said the other, feebly.

"What did you go to the police about me for, then?" demanded the skipper.

"Me?" said the mate, in the shrill accents of astonishment. "Me? I didn't go to no police about you. Why should I?"

"Do you mean to say you didn't report my absence last night to the police?" said the skipper, sternly.

"Cert'nly not," said the mate, plucking up courage. "Why should I? If you like to take a night off it's nothing to do with me. I 'ope I know my duty better. I don't know what you're talking about."

"And the police haven't been watching the ship and inquiring for me?" asked the skipper.

The mate shook his bewildered head. "Why should they?" he inquired.

The skipper made no reply. He sat goggle-eyed, staring straight before him, trying in vain to realize the hardness of the heart that had been responsible for such a scurvy trick.

"Besides, it ain't the fust time you've been out all night," remarked the mate, aggressively.

The skipper favored him with a glance the dignity of which was somewhat impaired by his complexion, and in a slow and stately fashion ascended to the deck. Then he caught his breath sharply and paled beneath the coaldust as he saw Sergeant Pilbeam standing on the quay, opposite the ship. By his side stood Miss Pilbeam, and both, with a far-away look in their eyes, were smiling vaguely but contentedly at the horizon. The sergeant appeared to be the first to see the skipper.

"Ahoy, Darkie!" he cried.

Captain Bligh, who was creeping slowly aft, halted, and, clenching his fists, regarded him ferociously.

"Give this to the skipper, will you, my lad?" said the sergeant, holding up the jacket Bligh had left behind. "Good-looking young man with a very fine moustache he is."

"Was," said his daughter, in a mournful voice.

"And a rather dark complexion," continued the sergeant, grinning madly. "I was going to take him— for stealing my coal—but I thought better of it. Thought of a better way. At least, my daughter did. So long; Darkie."

He kissed the top of a fat middle finger, and, turning away, walked off with Miss Pilbeam. The skipper stood watching them with his head swimming until, arrived at the corner, they stopped and the sergeant came slowly back.

"I was nearly forgetting," he said, slowly. "Tell your skipper that if so be as he wants to apologize— for stealing my coal—I shall be at home at tea at five o'clock."

He jerked his thumb in the direction of Miss Pilbeam and winked with slow deliberation. "She'll be there, too," he added. "Savvy?"

SHAREHOLDERS

Sailor man—said the night-watchman, musingly—a sailorman is like a fish he is safest when 'e is at sea. When a fish comes ashore it is in for trouble, and so is sailorman. One poor chap I knew 'ardly ever came ashore without getting married; and he was found out there was no less than six wimmen in the court all taking away 'is character at once. And when he spoke up Solomon the magistrate pretty near bit 'is 'ead off.

Then look at the trouble they get in with their money! They come ashore from a long trip, smelling of it a'most, and they go from port to port like a lord. Everybody has got their eye on that money— everybody except the sailorman, that is—and afore he knows wot's 'appened, and who 'as got it, he's looking for a ship agin. When he ain't robbed of 'is money, he wastes it; and when 'e don't do either, he loses it.

I knew one chap who hid 'is money. He'd been away ten months, and, knowing 'ow easy money goes, 'e made up sixteen pounds in a nice little parcel and hid it where nobody could find it. That's wot he said, and p'r'aps 'e was right. All I know is, he never found it. I did the same thing myself once with a couple o' quid I ran acrost unexpected, on'y, unfortunately for me, I hid it the day afore my missus started 'er spring-cleaning.

One o' the worst men I ever knew for getting into trouble when he came ashore was old Sam Small. If he couldn't find it by 'imself, Ginger Dick and Peter Russet would help 'im look for it. Generally speaking they found it without straining their eyesight.

I remember one time they was home, arter being away pretty near a year, and when they was paid off they felt like walking gold-mines. They went about smiling all over with good-temper and 'appiness, and for the first three days they was like brothers. That didn't last, of course, and on the fourth day Sam Small, arter saying wot 'e would do to Ginger and Peter if it wasn't for the police, went off by 'imself.

His temper passed off arter a time, and 'e began to look cheerful agin. It was a lovely morning, and, having nothing to do and plenty in 'is pocket to do it with, he went along like a schoolboy with a 'arf holiday. He went as far as Stratford on the top of a tram for a mouthful o' fresh air, and came back to his favourite coffee-shop with a fine appetite for dinner. There was a very nice gentlemanly chap sitting opposite 'im, and the way he begged Sam's pardon for splashing gravy over 'im made Sam take a liking to him at once. Nicely dressed he was, with a gold pin in 'is tie, and a fine gold watch-chain acrost his weskit; and Sam could see he 'ad been brought up well by the way he used 'is knife and fork. He kept looking at Sam in a thoughtful kind o' way, and at last he said wot a beautiful morning it was, and wot a fine day it must be in the, country. In a little while they began to talk like a couple of old friends, and he told Sam all about 'is father, wot was a clergyman in the country, and Sam talked about a father of his as was living private on three 'undred a year.

"Ah, money's a useful thing," ses the man.

"It ain't everything," ses Sam. "It won't give you 'appiness. I've run through a lot in my time, so I ought to know."

"I expect you've got a bit left, though," ses the man, with a wink.

Sam laughed and smacked 'is pocket. "I've got a trifle to go on with," he ses, winking back. "I never feel comfortable without a pound or two in my pocket."

"You look as though you're just back from a vy'ge," ses the man, looking at 'im very hard.

"I am," ses Sam, nodding. "Just back arter ten months, and I'm going to spend a bit o' money afore I sign on agin, I can tell you."

"That's wot it was given to us for," ses the man, nodding at him.

They both got up to go at the same time and walked out into the street together, and, when Sam asked 'im whether he might have the pleasure of standing 'im a drink, he said he might. He talked about the different kinds of drink as they walked along till Sam, wot was looking for a high-class pub, got such a raging thirst on 'im he hardly knew wot to do with 'imself. He passed several pubs, and walked on as fast as he could to the Three Widders.

"Do you want to go in there partikler?" ses the man, stopping at the door.

"No," ses Sam, staring.

"'Cos I know a place where they sell the best glass o' port wine in London," ses the man.

He took Sam up two or three turnings, and then led him into a quiet little pub in a back street. There was a cosy little saloon bar with nobody in it, and, arter Sam had 'ad two port wines for the look of the thing, he 'ad a pint o' six-ale because he liked it. His new pal had one too, and he 'ad just taken a pull at it and wiped his mouth, when 'e noticed a little bill pinned up at the back of the bar.

"*Lost, between—the Mint and—Tower Stairs,*" he ses, leaning forward and reading very slow, "*a gold—locket—set with—diamonds. Whoever will—return—the same to—Mr. Smith—Orange Villa—Barnet—will receive —thirty pounds—reward.*"

"'Ow much?" ses Sam, starting. "Thirty pounds," ses the man. "Must be a good locket. Where'd you get that?" he ses, turning to the barmaid.

"Gentleman came in an hour ago," ses the gal, "and, arter he had 'ad two or three drinks with the guv'nor, he asks 'im to stick it up. 'Arf crying he was—said 'it 'ad belonged to his old woman wot died."

She went off to serve a customer at the other end of the bar wot was making little dents in it with his pot, and the man came back and sat down by Sam agin, and began to talk about horse-racing. At least, he tried to, but Sam couldn't talk of nothing but that locket, and wot a nice steady sailorman could do with thirty pounds.

"Well, p'r'aps you'll find it," ses the man, chaffing-like. "'Ave another pint."

Sam had one, but it only made 'im more solemn, and he got in quite a temper as 'e spoke about casuals loafing about on Tower Hill with their 'ands in their pockets, and taking gold lockets out of the mouths of hard-working sailormen.

"It mightn't be found yet," ses the man, speaking thoughtful-like. "It's wonderful how long a thing'll lay sometimes. Wot about going and 'aving a look for it?"

Sam shook his 'ead at fust, but arter turning the thing over in his mind, and 'aving another look at the bill, and copying down the name and address for luck, 'e said p'r'aps they might as well walk that way as anywhere else.

"Something seems to tell me we've got a chance," ses the man, as they stepped outside.

"It's a funny feeling and I can't explain it, but it always means good luck. Last time I had it an aunt o' mine swallered 'er false teeth and left me five 'undred pounds."

"There's aunts and aunts," ses Sam, grunting. "I 'ad one once, but if she had swallered 'er teeth she'd ha' been round to me to help 'er buy some new ones. That's the sort she was."

"Mind!" ses the man, patting 'im on the shoulder, "if we do find this, I don't want any of it. I've got all I want. It's all for you."

They went on like a couple o' brothers arter that, especially Sam, and when they got to the Mint they walked along slow down Tower Hill looking for the locket. It was awkward work, because, if people saw them looking about, they'd 'ave started looking too, and twice Sam nearly fell over owing to walking like a man with a stiff neck and squinting down both sides of his nose at once. When they got as far as the Stairs they came back on the other side of the road, and they 'ad turned to go back agin when a docker-looking chap stopped Sam's friend and spoke to 'im.

"I've got no change, my man," ses Sam's pal, pushing past him.

"I ain't begging, guv'nor," ses the chap, follering 'im up. "I'm trying to sell some-thing."

"Wot is it?" ses the other, stopping.

The man looked up and down the street, and then he put his 'ead near them and whispered.

"Eh?" ses Sam's pal.

"Something I picked up," ses the man, still a-whispering.

Sam got a pinch on the arm from 'is pal that nearly made him scream, then they both stood still, staring at the docker.

"Wot is it?" ses Sam, at last.

The docker looked over his shoulder agin, and then 'e put his 'and in his trouser-pocket and just showed 'em a big, fat gold locket with diamonds stuck all over it. Then he shoved it back in 'is pocket, while Sam's pal was giving 'im a pinch worse than wot the other was.

"It's the one," he ses, in a whisper. "Let's 'ave another look at it," he ses to the docker.

The man fished it out of his pocket agin, and held on to it tight while they looked at it.

"Where did you find it?" ses Sam.

"Found it over there, just by the Mint," ses the man, pointing.

"Wot d'ye want for it?" ses Sam's pal.

"As much as I can get," ses the man. "I don't quite know 'ow much it's worth, that's the worst of it. Wot d'ye say to twenty pounds, and chance it?"

Sam laughed—the sort of laugh a pal 'ad once give him a black eye for.

"Twenty pounds!" he ses; "twenty pounds! 'Ave you gorn out of your mind, or wot? I'll give you a couple of quid for it."

"Well, it's all right, captin," ses the man, "there's no 'arm done. I'll try somebody else—or p'r'aps there'll be a big reward for it. I don't believe it was bought for a 'undred pounds."

He was just sheering off when Sam's pal caught 'im by the arm and asked him to let 'im have another look at it. Then he came back to Sam and led 'im a little way off, whispering to 'im that it was the chance of a life time.

"And if you prefer to keep it for a little while and then sell it, instead of getting the reward for it, I dare say it would be worth a hundred pounds to you," 'e ses.

"I ain't got twenty pounds," ses Sam.

"'Ow much 'ave you got?" ses his pal.

Sam felt in 'is pockets, and the docker came up and stood watching while he counted it. Altogether it was nine pounds fourteen shillings and tuppence.

"P'r'aps you've got some more at 'ome," ses his pal.

"Not a farthing," ses Sam, which was true as far as the farthing went.

"Or p'r'aps you could borrer some," ses his pal, in a soft, kind voice. "I'd lend it to you with pleasure, on'y I haven't got it with me."

Sam shook his 'ead, and at last, arter the docker 'ad said he wouldn't let it go for less than twenty, even to save 'is life, he let it go for the nine pounds odd, a silver watch-chain, two cigars wot Sam 'ad been sitting on by mistake, and a sheath-knife.

"Shove it in your pocket and don't let a soul see it," ses the man, handing over the locket. "I might as well give it away a'most. But it can't be 'elped."

He went off up the 'ill shaking his 'ead, and Sam's pal, arter watching him for a few seconds, said good-bye in a hurry and went off arter 'im to tell him to keep 'is mouth shut about it.

Sam walked back to his lodgings on air, as the saying is, and even did a little bit of a skirt-dance to a pianner-organ wot was playing. Peter and Ginger was out, and so was his land-lady, a respectable woman as was minding the rest of 'is money for him, and when he asked 'er little gal, a kid of eleven, to trust 'im for some tin she gave 'im a lecture on wasting his money instead wot took 'is breath away—all but a word or two.

He got some of 'is money from his landlady at eight o'clock, arter listening to 'er for 'arf an hour, and then he 'ad to pick it up off of the floor, and say "Thank you" for it.

He went to bed afore Ginger and Peter came in, but 'e was so excited he couldn't sleep, and long arter they was in bed he laid there and thought of all the different ways of spending a 'undred pounds. He kept taking the locket from under 'is piller and feeling it; then he felt 'e must 'ave another look at it, and arter coughing 'ard two or three times and calling out to the other two not to snore—to see if they was awake—he got out o' bed and lit the candle. Ginger and Peter was both fast asleep, with their eyes screwed up and their mouths wide open, and 'e sat on the bed and looked at the locket until he was a'most dazzled.

"'Ullo, Sam!" ses a voice. "Wot 'ave you got there?"

Sam nearly fell off the bed with surprise and temper. Then 'e hid the locket in his 'and and blew out the candle.

"Who gave it to you?" ses Ginger.

"You get off to sleep, and mind your own bisness," ses Sam, grinding 'is teeth.

He got back into bed agin and laid there listening to Ginger waking up Peter. Peter woke up disagreeable, but when Ginger told 'im that Sam 'ad stole a gold locket as big as a saucer, covered with diamonds, he altered 'is mind.

"Let's 'ave a look at it," he ses, sitting up.

"Ginger's dreaming," ses Sam, in a shaky voice. "I ain't got no locket. Wot d'you think I want a locket for?"

Ginger got out o' bed and lit the candle agin. "Come on!" he ses, "let's 'ave a look at it. I wasn't dreaming. I've been awake all the time, watching you."

Sam shut 'is eyes and turned his back to them.

"He's gone to sleep, pore old chap," ses Ginger. "We'll 'ave a look at it without waking 'im. You take that side, Peter! Mind you don't disturb 'im."

He put his 'and in under the bed-clo'es and felt all up and down Sam's back, very careful. Sam stood it for 'arf a minute, and then 'e sat up in bed and behaved more like a windmill than a man.

"Hold his 'ands," ses Ginger.

"Hold 'em yourself," ses Peter, dabbing 'is nose with his shirt-sleeve.

"Well, we're going to see it," ses Ginger, "if we have to make enough noise to rouse the 'ouse. Fust of all we're going to ask you perlite; then we shall get louder and louder. *Show us the locket wot you stole, Sam!*"

"Show—us—the—diamond locket!" ses Peter.

"It's my turn, Peter," ses Ginger. "One, two, three. SHOW—US—TH'—"

"Shut up," ses Sam, trembling all over. "I'll show it to you if you stop your noise."

He put his 'and under his piller, but afore he showed it to 'em he sat up in bed and made 'em a little speech. He said 'e never wanted to see their faces agin as long as he lived, and why Ginger's mother 'adn't put 'im in a pail o' cold water when 'e was born 'e couldn't understand. He said 'e didn't believe that even a mother could love a baby that looked like a cod-fish with red 'air, and as for Peter Russet, 'e believed his mother died of fright.

"That'll do," ses Ginger, as Sam stopped to get 'is breath. "Are you going to show us the locket, or 'ave we got to shout agin?"

Sam swallered something that nearly choked 'im, and then he opened his 'and and showed it to them. Peter told 'im to wave it so as they could see the diamonds flash, and then Ginger waved the candle to see 'ow they looked that way, and pretty near set pore Sam's whiskers on fire.

They didn't leave 'im alone till they knew as much about it as he could tell 'em, and they both of 'em told 'im that if he took a reward of thirty pounds for it, instead of selling it for a 'undred, he was a bigger fool than he looked.

"I shall turn it over in my mind," ses Sam, sucking 'is teeth. "When I want your advice I'll ask you for it."

"We wasn't thinking of you," ses Ginger; "we was thinking of ourselves."

"You!" ses Sam, with a bit of a start. "Wot's it got to do with you?"

"Our share'll be bigger, that's all," ses Ginger.

"Much bigger," ses Peter. "I couldn't dream of letting it go at thirty. It's chucking money away. Why, we might get *two* 'undred for it. Who knows?"

Sam sat on the edge of 'is bed like a man in a dream, then 'e began to make a noise like a cat with a fish-bone in its throat, and then 'e stood up and let fly.

"Don't stop 'im, Peter," ses Ginger. "Let 'im go on; it'll do him good."

"He's forgot all about that penknife you picked up and went shares in," ses Peter. "I wouldn't be mean for *twenty* lockets."

"Nor me neither," ses Ginger. "But we won't let 'im be mean—for 'is own sake. We'll 'ave our rights."

"Rights!" ses Sam. "Rights! You didn't find it."

"We always go shares if we find anything," ses Ginger. "Where's your memory, Sam?" "But I didn't find it," ses Sam.

"No, you bought it," ses Peter, "and if you don't go shares we'll split on you—see? Then you can't sell it anyway, and perhaps you won't even get the reward. We can be at Orange Villa as soon as wot you can."

"Sooner," ses Ginger, nodding. "But there's no need to do that. If 'e don't go shares I'll slip round to the police-station fust thing in the morning."

"You know the way there all right," ses Sam, very bitter.

"And we don't want none o' your back-answers," ses Ginger. "Are you going shares or not?"

"Wot about the money I paid for it?" ses Sam, "and my trouble?"

Ginger and Peter sat down on the bed to talk it over, and at last, arter calling themselves a lot o' bad names for being too kind-'earted, they offered 'im five pounds each for their share in the locket.

"And that means you've got your share for next to nothing, Sam," ses Ginger.

"Some people wouldn't 'ave given you any-thing," ses Peter.

Sam gave way at last, and then 'e stood by making nasty remarks while Ginger wrote out a paper for them all to sign, because he said he had known Sam such a long time.

It was a'most daylight afore they got to sleep, and the fust thing Ginger did when he woke was to wake Sam up, and offer to shake 'ands with him. The noise woke Peter up, and, as Sam wouldn't shake 'ands with 'im either, they both patted him on the back instead.

They made him take 'em to the little pub, arter breakfast, to read the bill about the reward. Sam didn't mind going, as it 'appened, as he 'oped to meet 'is new pal there and tell 'im his troubles, but, though they stayed there some time, 'e didn't turn up. He wasn't at the coffee-shop for dinner, neither.

Peter and Ginger was in 'igh spirits, and, though Sam told 'em plain that he would sooner walk about with a couple of real pickpockets, they wouldn't leave 'im an inch.

"Anybody could steal it off of you, Sam," ses Ginger, patting 'im on the weskit to make sure the locket was still there. "It's a good job you've got us to look arter you."

"We must buy 'im a money-belt with a pocket in it," ses Peter.

Ginger nodded at 'im. "Yes," he ses, "that would be safer. And he'd better wear it next to 'is skin, with everything over it. I should feel more comfortable then."

"And wot about me?" says Sam, turning on 'im.

"Well, we'll take it in turns," ses Ginger. "You one day, and then me, and then Peter."

Sam gave way at last, as arter all he could see it was the safest thing to do, but he 'ad so much to say about it that they got fair sick of the sound of 'is voice. They 'ad to go 'ome for 'im to put the belt on; and then at seven o'clock in the evening, arter Sam had 'ad two or three pints, they had to go 'ome agin, 'cos he was complaining of tight-lacing.

Ginger had it on next day and he went 'ome five times. The other two went with 'im in case he lost 'imself, and stood there making nasty remarks while he messed 'imself up with a penn'orth of cold cream. It was a cheap belt, and pore Ginger said that, when they 'ad done with it, it would come in handy for sand-paper.

Peter didn't like it any better than the other two did, and twice they 'ad to speak to 'im about stopping in the street and trying to make 'imself more comfortable by wriggling. Sam said people misunderstood it.

Arter that they agreed to wear it outside their shirt, and even then Ginger said it scratched 'im. And every day they got more and more worried about wot was the best thing to do with the locket, and whether it would be safe to try and sell it. The idea o' walking about with a fortune in their pockets that they couldn't spend a'most drove 'em crazy.

"The longer we keep it, the safer it'll be," ses Sam, as they was walking down Hounds-ditch one day.

"We'll sell it when I'm sixty," ses Ginger, nasty-like.

"Then old Sam won't be 'ere to have 'is share," ses Peter.

Sam was just going to answer 'em back, when he stopped and began to smile instead. Straight in front of 'im was the gentleman he 'ad met in the coffee-shop, coming along with another man, and he just 'ad time to see that it was the docker who 'ad sold him the locket, when they both saw 'im. They turned like a flash, and, afore Sam could get 'is breath, bolted up a little alley and disappeared.

"Wot's the row?" ses Ginger, staring.

Sam didn't answer 'im. He stood there struck all of a heap.

"Do you know 'em?" ses Peter.

Sam couldn't answer 'im for a time. He was doing a bit of 'ard thinking.

"Chap I 'ad a row with the other night," he ses, at last.

He walked on very thoughtful, and the more 'e thought, the less 'e liked it. He was so pale that Ginger thought 'e was ill and advised 'im to 'ave a drop o' brandy. Peter recommended rum, so to please 'em he 'ad both. It brought 'is colour back, but not 'is cheerfulness.

He gave 'em both the slip next morning; which was easy, as Ginger was wearing the locket, and, arter fust 'aving a long ride for nothing owing to getting in the wrong train, he got to Barnet.

It was a big place; big enough to 'ave a dozen Orange Villas, but pore Sam couldn't find one. It wasn't for want of trying neither.

He asked at over twenty shops, and the post-office, and even went to the police-station. He must ha' walked six or seven miles looking for it, and at last, 'arf ready to drop, 'e took the train back.

He 'ad some sausages and mashed potatoes with a pint o' stout at a place in Bishopsgate, and then 'e started to walk 'ome. The only comfort he 'ad was the thought of the ten pounds Ginger and Peter 'ad paid 'im; and when he remembered that he began to cheer up and even smile. By the time he got 'ome 'e was beaming all over 'is face.

"Where've you been?" ses Ginger.

"Enjoying myself by myself," ses Sam.

"Please yourself," ses Peter, very severe, "but where'd you ha' been if we 'ad sold the locket and skipped, eh?"

"You wouldn't 'ave enjoyed yourself by yourself then," ses Ginger. "Yes, you may laugh!"

Sam didn't answer 'im, but he sat down on 'is bed and 'is shoulders shook till Ginger lost his temper and gave him a couple o' thumps on the back that pretty near broke it.

"All right," ses Sam, very firm. "Now you 'ave done for yourselves. I 'ad a'most made up my mind to go shares; now you sha'n't 'ave a ha'penny."

Ginger laughed then. "Ho!" he ses, "and 'ow are you going to prevent it?"

"We've got the locket, Sam," ses Peter, smiling and shaking his 'ead at 'im.

"And we'll mind it till it's sold," ses Ginger.

Sam laughed agin, short and nasty. Then he undressed 'imself very slow and got into bed. At twelve o'clock, just as Ginger was dropping off, he began to laugh agin, and 'e only stopped when 'e heard Ginger getting out of bed to 'im.

He stayed in bed next morning, 'cos he said 'is sides was aching, but 'e laughed agin as they was going out, and when they came back he 'ad gorn.

We never know 'ow much we' like anything till we lose it. A week arterwards, as Ginger was being 'elped out of a pawnshop by Peter, he said 'e would give all he 'adn't got for the locket to be near enough to Sam to hear 'im laugh agin.

SKILLED ASSISTANCE

The night-watchman, who had left his seat on the jetty to answer the gate-bell, came back with disgust written on a countenance only too well designed to express it.

"If she's been up 'ere once in the last week to, know whether the *Silvia* is up she's been four or five times," he growled. "He's forty-seven if he's a day; 'is left leg is shorter than 'is right, and he talks with a stutter. When she's with 'im you'd think as butter wouldn't melt in 'er mouth; but the way she talked to me just now you'd think I was paid a-purpose to wait on her. I asked 'er at last wot she thought I was here for, and she said she didn't know, and nobody else neither. And afore she went off she told the potman from the 'Albion,' wot was listening, that I was known all over Wapping as the Sleeping Beauty.

"She ain't the fust I've 'ad words with, not by a lot. They're all the same; they all start in a nice, kind, soapy sort o' way, and, as soon as they don't get wot they want, fly into a temper and ask me who, I think I am. I told one woman once not to be silly, and I shall never forget it as long as I live-never. For all I know, she's wearing a bit o' my 'air in a locket to this day, and very likely boasting that I gave it to her.

"Talking of her reminds me of another woman. There was a Cap'n Pinner, used to trade between 'ere and Hull on a schooner named the Snipe. Nice little craft she was, and 'e was a very nice feller. Many and many's the pint we've 'ad together, turn and turn-about, and the on'y time we ever 'ad a cross word was when somebody hid his clay pipe in my beer and 'e was foolish enough to think I'd done it.

"He 'ad a nice little cottage, 'e told me about, near Hull, and 'is wife's father, a man of pretty near seventy, lived with 'em. Well-off the old man was, and, as she was his only daughter, they looked to 'ave all his money when he'd gorn. Their only fear was that 'e might marry agin, and, judging from wot 'e used to tell me about the old man, I thought it more than likely.

"'If it wasn't for my missis he'd ha' been married over and over agin,' he ses one day. 'He's like a child playing with gunpowder.'

"''Ow would it be to let 'im burn hisself a bit?' I ses.

"'If you was to see some o' the gunpowder he wants to play with, you wouldn't talk like that,' ses the cap'n. 'You'd know better. The on'y thing is to keep 'em apart, and my pore missis is wore to a shadder a-doing of it.'

"It was just about a month arter that that he brought the old man up to London with 'im. They 'ad some stuff to put out at Smith's Wharf, t'other side of the river, afore they came to us, and though they was on'y there four or five days, it was long enough for that old man to get into trouble.

"The skipper told me about it ten minutes arter they was made snug in the inner berth 'ere. He walked up and down like a man with a raging toothache, and arter follering 'im up and down the wharf till I was tired out, I discovered that 'is father-in-law 'ad got 'imself mixed up with a widder-woman ninety years old and weighing twenty stun. Arter he 'ad cooled down a bit, and I 'ad given 'im a few little pats on the shoulder, 'e made it forty-eight years old and fourteen stun.

"'He's getting ready to go and meet her now,' he ses, 'and wot my missis'll say to me, I don't know.'

"His father-in-law came up on deck as 'e spoke, and began to brush 'imself all over with a clothesbrush. Nice-looking little man 'e was, with blue eyes, and a little white beard, cut to a point, and dressed up in a serge suit with brass buttons, and a white yachting cap. His real name was Mr. Finch, but the skipper called 'im Uncle Dick, and he took such a fancy to me that in five minutes I was calling 'im Uncle Dick too.

"'Time I was moving,' he ses, by and by. 'I've got an app'intment.'

"'Oh! who with?' ses the skipper, pretending not to know.

"'Friend o' mine, in the army,' ses the old man, with a wink at me. 'So long.'

"He went off as spry as a boy, and as soon as he'd gorn the skipper started walking back'ards and for'ards agin, and raving.

"'Let's 'ope as he's on'y amusing 'imself,' I ses.

"'Wait till you see 'er,' ses the skipper; 'then you won't talk foolishness.'

"As it 'appened she came back with Uncle Dick that evening, to see 'im safe, and I see at once wot sort of a woman it was. She 'adn't been on the wharf five minutes afore you'd ha' thought it belonged to 'er, and when she went and sat on the schooner it seemed to be about 'arf its size. She called the skipper Tom, and sat there as cool as you please holding Uncle Dick's 'and, and patting it.

"I took the skipper round to the 'Bull's Head' arter she 'ad gorn, and I wouldn't let 'im say a word until he had 'ad two pints. He felt better then, and some o' the words 'e used surprised me.

"'Wot's to be done?' he ses at last. 'You see 'ow it is, Bill.'

"'Can't you get 'im away?' I ses. 'Who is she, and wot's 'er name?'

"'Her name,' ses the skipper, 'her name is Jane Maria Elizabeth Muffit, and she lives over at Rotherhithe.'

"'She's very likely married already,' I ses.

"'Her 'usband died ten years ago,' ses the skipper; 'passed away in 'is sleep. Overlaid, I should say.'

"He sat there smoking, and I sat there thinking. Twice 'e spoke to me, and I held my 'and up and said 'H'sh.' Then I turned to 'im all of a sudden and pinched his arm so hard he nearly dropped 'is beer.

"'Is Uncle Dick a nervous man?' I ses.

"'Nervous is no name for it,' he ses, staring.

"'Very good, then,' I ses. 'I'll send 'er husband to frighten 'im.'

"The skipper looked at me very strange. 'Yes,' he ses. 'Yes. Yes.'

"'Frighten 'im out of 'is boots, and make him give 'er up,' I ses. 'Or better still, get 'im to run away and go into hiding for a time. That 'ud be best, in case 'e found out.'

"'Found out wot?' ses the skipper.

"'Found out it wasn't 'er husband,' I ses.

"'Bill,' ses the skipper, very earnest, 'this is the fust beer I've 'ad to-day, and I wish I could say the same for you.'

"I didn't take 'im at fast, but when I did I gave a laugh that brought in two more customers to see wot was the matter. Then I took 'im by the arm—arter a little trouble—and, taking 'im back to the wharf, explained my meaning to 'im.

"'I know the very man,' I ses. 'He comes into a public-'ouse down my way sometimes. Artful 'Arry, he's called, and, for 'arf-a-quid, say, he'd frighten Uncle Dick 'arf to death. He's big and ugly, and picks up a living by selling meerschaum pipes he's found to small men wot don't want 'em. Wonderful gift o' the gab he's got.'

"We went acrost to the 'Albion' to talk it over. There's several bars there, and the landlady always keeps cotton-wool in 'er ears, not 'aving been brought up to the public line. The skipper told me all 'e knew about Mrs. Muffit, and we arranged that Artful 'Arry should come down at seven o'clock next night, if so be as I could find 'im in time.

"I got up early the next arternoon, and as it 'appened, he came into the 'Duke of Edinburgh' five minutes arter I got there. Nasty temper 'e was in, too. He'd just found a meerschaum pipe, as usual, and the very fust man 'e tried to sell it to said that it was the one 'e lost last Christmas, and gave 'im a punch in the jaw for it.

"'He's a thief, that's wot he is,' ses 'Arry; 'and I 'ate thiefs. 'Ow's a honest tradesman to make a living when there's people like that about?'

"I stood 'im 'arf a pint, and though it hurt 'im awful to drink it, he said 'ed 'ave another just to see if he could bear the pain. Arter he had 'ad three 'e began for to take a more cheerful view o' life, and told me about a chap that spent three weeks in the London 'Orsepittle for calling 'im a liar.

"'Treat me fair,' he ses, 'and I'll treat other people fair. I never broke my word without a good reason for it, and that's more than everybody can say. If I told you the praise I've 'ad from some people you wouldn't believe it.'

"I let 'im go on till he 'ad talked 'imself into a good temper, and then I told 'im of the little job I 'ad got for 'im. He listened quiet till I 'ad finished, and then he shook 'is 'ead.

"'It ain't in my line,' he ses.

"'There's 'arf a quid 'anging to it,' I ses.

"'Arry shook his 'ead agin. 'Tain't enough, mate,' he ses. 'If you was to make it a quid I won't say as I mightn't think of it.'

"I 'ad told the skipper that it might cost 'im a quid, so I knew 'ow far I could go; and at last, arter 'Arry 'ad got as far as the door three times, I gave way.

"'And I'll 'ave it now,' he ses, 'to prevent mistakes.'

"'No, 'Arry,' I ses, very firm. 'Besides, it ain't my money, you see.'

"'You mean to say you don't trust me,' 'e ses, firing up.

"'I'd trust you with untold gold,' I ses, 'but not with a real quid; you're too fond of a joke, 'Arry.'

"We 'ad another long argyment about it, and I had to tell 'im plain at last that when I wanted to smell 'is fist, I'd say so.

"'You turn up at the wharf at five minutes to seven,' I ses, 'and I'll give you ten bob of it; arter you've done your business I'll give you the other. Come along quiet, and you'll see me waiting at the gate for you.'

"He gave way arter a time, and, fust going 'ome for a cup o' tea, I went on to the wharf to tell the skipper 'ow things stood.

"'It couldn't 'ave 'appened better,' he ses. 'Uncle Dick is sure to be aboard at that time, 'cos 'e's going acrost the water at eight o'clock to pay 'er a visit. And all the hands'll be away. I've made sure of that.'

"He gave me the money for Artful 'Arry in two 'arf-suverins, and then we went over to the 'Albion' for a quiet glass and a pipe, and to wait for seven o'clock.

"I left 'im there at ten minutes to, and at five minutes to, punctual to the minute, I see 'Arry coming along swinging a thick stick with a knob on the end of it.

"'Where's the 'arf thick-un?' he ses, looking round to see that the coast was clear.

"I gave it to 'im, and arter biting it in three places and saying it was a bit short in weight he dropped it in 'is weskit-pocket and said 'e was ready.

"I left 'im there for a minute while I went and 'ad a look round. The deck of the Snipe was empty, but I could 'ear Uncle Dick down in the cabin singing; and, arter listening for a few seconds to make sure that it was singing, I went back and beckoned to 'Arry.

"'He's down in the cabin,' I ses, pointing. 'Don't overdo it, 'Arry, and at the same time don't underdo it, as you might say.'

"'I know just wot you want,' ses 'Arry, 'and if you'd got the 'art of a man in you, you'd make it two quids.'

"He climbed on board and stood listening for a moment at the companion, and then 'e went down, while I went off outside the gate, so as to be out of earshot in case Uncle Dick called for me. I knew that I should 'ear all about wot went on arterwards—and I did.

"Artful 'Arry went down the companion-ladder very quiet, and then stood at the foot of it looking at Uncle Dick. He looked 'im up and down and all over, and then 'e gave a fierce, loud cough.

"'Good-evening,' he ses.

"'Good-evening,' ses Uncle Dick, staring at 'im. 'Did you want to see anybody?'

"'I did,' ses 'Arry. 'I do. And when I see 'im I'm going to put my arms round 'im and twist 'is neck; then I'm going to break every bone in 'is body, and arter that I'm going to shy 'im overboard to pison the fishes with.'

"'Dear me!' ses Uncle Dick, shifting away as far as 'e could.

"'I ain't 'ad a wink o' sleep for two nights,' ses 'Arry—'not ever since I 'eard of it. When I think of all I've done for that woman-working for 'er, and such-like-my blood boils. When I think of her passing 'erself off as a widder—my widder—and going out with another man, I don't know wot to do with myself.'

"Uncle Dick started and turned pale. Fust 'e seemed as if 'e was going to speak, and then 'e thought better of it. He sat staring at 'Arry as if 'e couldn't believe his eyes.

"'Wot would you do with a man like that?' ses 'Arry. 'I ask you, as man to man, wot would you do to 'im?'

"'P'r'aps-p'r'aps 'e didn't know,' ses Uncle Dick, stammering.

"'Didn't know!' ses 'Arry. 'Don't care, you mean. We've got a nice little 'ome, and, just because I've 'ad to leave it and lay low for a bit for knifing a man, she takes advantage of it. And it ain't the fust time, neither. Wot's the matter?'

"'Touch-touch of ague; I get it sometimes,' ses Uncle Dick.

"'I want to see this man Finch,' ses 'Arry, shaking 'is knobby stick. 'Muffit, my name is, and I want to tell 'im so.'

"Uncle Dick nearly shook 'imself on to the floor.

"'I—I'll go and see if 'e's in the fo'c'sle,' he ses at last.

"'He ain't there, 'cos I've looked,' ses 'Arry, 'arf shutting 'is eyes and looking at 'im hard. 'Wot might your name be?'

"'My name's Finch,' ses Uncle Dick, putting out his 'ands to keep him off; 'but I thought she was a widder. She told me her 'usband died ten years ago; she's deceived me as well as you. I wouldn't ha' dreamt of taking any notice of 'er if I'd known. Truth, I wouldn't. I should'nt ha' dreamt of such a thing.'

"Artful 'Arry played with 'is stick a little, and stood looking at 'im with a horrible look on 'is face.

"''Ow am I to know you're speaking the truth?' he ses, very slow. 'Eh? 'Ow can you prove it?'

"'If it was the last word I was to speak I'd say the same,' ses Uncle Dick. 'I tell you, I am as innercent as a new-born babe.'

"'If that's true,' ses 'Arry, 'she's deceived both of us. Now, if I let you go will you go straight off and bring her 'ere to me?'

"'I will,' ses Uncle Dick, jumping up.

""Arf a mo,' ses 'Arry, holding up 'is stick very quick. 'One thing is, if you don't come back, I'll 'ave you another day. I can't make up my mind wot to do. I can't think—I ain't tasted food for two days. If I 'ad any money in my pocket I'd 'ave a bite while you're gone.'

"'Why not get something?' ses Uncle Dick, putting his 'and in his pocket, in a great 'urry to please him, and pulling out some silver.

"'Arry said 'e would, and then he stood on one side to let 'im pass, and even put the knobby stick under 'im to help 'im up the companion-ladder.

"Uncle Dick passed me two minutes arterwards without a word, and set off down the road as fast as 'is little legs 'ud carry 'im. I watched 'im out o' sight, and then I went on board the schooner to see how 'Arry 'ad got on.

"Arry,' I ses, when he 'ad finished, 'you're a masterpiece!'

"'I know I am,' he ses. 'Wot about that other 'arf-quid?'

"'Here it is,' I ses, giving it to 'im. 'Fair masterpiece, that's wot you are. They may well call you Artful. Shake 'ands.'

"I patted 'im on the shoulder arter we 'ad shook 'ands, and we stood there smiling at each other and paying each other compliments.

"'Fancy 'em sitting 'ere and waiting for you to come back from that bite,' I ses.

"'I ought to 'ave 'ad more off of him,' ses 'Arry. "Owever, it can't be helped. I think I'll 'ave a lay down for a bit; I'm tired.'

"'Better be off,' I ses, shaking my 'ead. 'Time passes, and they might come back afore you think.'

"'Well, wot of it?' ses 'Arry.

"'Wot of it?' I ses. 'Why, it'ud spoil everything. It 'ud be blue ruin.'

"'Are you sure?' ses 'Arry'.

"'Sartin,' I ses.

"'Well, make it five quid, and I'll go, then,' he ses, sitting down agin.

"I couldn't believe my ears at fust, but when I could I drew myself up and told 'im wot I thought of 'im; and he sat there and laughed at me.

"'Why, you called me a masterpiece just now,' he ses. 'I shouldn't be much of a masterpiece if I let a chance like this slip. Why, I shouldn't be able to look myself in the face. Where's the skipper?'

"'Sitting in the "Albion",' I ses, 'arf choking.

"'Go and tell 'im it's five quid,' ses 'Arry. 'I don't mean five more, on'y four. Some people would ha' made it five, but I like to deal square and honest.'

"I run over for the skipper in a state of mind that don't bear thinking of, and he came back with me, 'arf crazy. When we got to the cabin we found the door was locked, and, arter the skipper 'ad told Artful wot he'd do to 'im if he didn't open it, he 'ad to go on deck and talk to 'im through the skylight.

"'If you ain't off of my ship in two twos,' he ses, 'I'll fetch a policeman.'

"'You go and fetch four pounds,' ses 'Arry; 'that's wot I'm waiting for, not a policeman. Didn't the watchman tell you?'

"'The bargain was for one pound,' ses the skipper, 'ardly able to speak.

"'Well, you tell that to the policeman,' ses Artful 'Arry.

"It was no use, he'd got us every way; and at last the skipper turns out 'is pockets, and he ses, 'Look 'ere,' he ses, 'I've got seventeen and tenpence ha' penny. Will you go if I give you that?'

"''Ow much has the watchman got?' ses 'Arry. 'His lodger lost 'is purse the other day.'

"I'd got two and ninepence, as it 'appened, and then there was more trouble because the skipper wouldn't give 'im the money till he 'ad gone, and 'e wouldn't go till he 'ad got it. The skipper gave way at last, and as soon as he 'ad got it 'Arry ses, 'Now 'op off and borrer the rest, and look slippy about it.'

"I put one hand over the skipper's mouth fust, and then, finding that was no good, I put the other. It was no good wasting bad langwidge on 'Arry.

"I pacified the skipper at last, and arter 'Arry 'ad swore true 'e'd go when 'e'd got the money, the skipper rushed round to try and raise it. It's a difficult job at the best o' times, and I sat there on the skylight shivering and wondering whether the skipper or Mrs. Muffit would turn up fust.

"Hours seemed to pass away, and then I see the wicket in the gate open, and the skipper come through. He jumped on deck without a word, and then, going over to the skylight, 'anded down the money to 'Arry.

"'Right-o,' ses 'Arry. 'It on'y shows you wot you can do by trying.'

"He unlocked the door and came up on deck, looking at us very careful, and playing with 'is stick.

"'You've got your money,' ses the skipper; 'now go as quick as you can.'

"'Arry smiled and nodded at him. Then he stepped on to the wharf and was just moving to the gate, with us follering, when the wicket opened and in came Mrs. Muffit and Uncle Dick.

"'There he is,' ses Uncle Dick. 'That's the man!'

"Mrs. Muffit walked up to 'im, and my 'art a'most stopped beating. Her face was the colour of beetroot with temper, and you could 'ave heard her breath fifty yards away.

"'Ho!' she says, planting 'erself in front of Artful 'Arry, 'so you're the man that ses you're my 'usband, are you?'

"'That's all right,' ses 'Arry, 'it's all a mistake.'

"'MISTAKE?' ses Mrs. Muffit.

"'Mistake o' Bill's,' ses 'Arry, pointing to me. 'I told 'im I thought 'e was wrong, but 'e would 'ave it. I've got a bad memory, so I left it to 'im.'

"'Ho!' ses Mrs. Muffit, taking a deep breath. 'Ho! I thought as much. Wot 'ave you got to say for yourself—eh?'

"She turned on me like a wild cat, with her 'ands in front of her. I've been scratched once in my life, and I wasn't going to be agin, so, fixing my eyes on 'er, I just stepped back a bit, ready for 'er. So long as I kept my eye fixed on 'ers she couldn't do anything. I knew that. Unfortunately I stepped back just a inch too far, and next moment I went over back'ards in twelve foot of water.

"Arter all, p'r'aps it was the best thing that could have 'appened to me; it stopped her talking. It ain't the fust time I've 'ad a wet jacket; but as for the skipper, and pore Uncle Dick—wot married her— they've been in hot water ever since."

THE SKIPPER OF THE "OSPREY"

It was a quarter to six in the morning as the mate of the sailing-barge Osprey came on deck and looked round for the master, who had been sleeping ashore and was somewhat overdue. Ten minutes passed before he appeared on the wharf, and the mate saw with surprise that he was leaning on the arm of a pretty girl of twenty, as he hobbled painfully down to the barge.

"Here you are then," said the mate, his face clearing. "I began to think you weren't coming."

"I'm not," said the skipper; "I've got the gout crool bad. My darter here's going to take my place, an' I'm going to take it easy in bed for a bit."

"I'll go an' make it for you," said the mate.

"I mean my bed at home," said the skipper sharply. "I want good nursing an' attention."

The mate looked puzzled.

"But you don't really mean to say this young lady is coming aboard instead of you?" he said.

"That's just what I do mean," said the skipper. "She knows as much about it as I do. She lived aboard with me until she was quite a big girl. You'll take your orders from her. What are you whistling about? Can't I do as I like about my own ship?"

"O' course you can," said the mate drily; "an' I s'pose I can whistle if I like—I never heard no orders against it."

"Gimme a kiss, Meg, an' git aboard," said the skipper, leaning on his stick and turning his cheek to his daughter, who obediently gave him a perfunctory kiss on the left eyebrow, and sprang lightly aboard the barge.

"Cast off," said she, in a business-like manner, as she seized a boat-hook and pushed off from the jetty. "Ta ta, Dad, and go straight home, mind; the cab's waiting."

"Ay, ay, my dear," said the proud father, his eye moistening with paternal pride as his daughter, throwing off her jacket, ran and assisted the mate with the sail. "Lord, what a fine boy she would have made!"

He watched the barge until she was well under way, and then, waving his hand to his daughter, crawled slowly back to the cab; and, being to a certain extent a believer in homeopathy, treated his complaint with a glass of rum.

"I'm sorry your father's so bad, miss," said the mate, who was still somewhat dazed by the recent proceedings, as the girl came up and took the wheel from him. "He was complaining a goodish bit all the way up."

"A wilful man must have his way," said Miss Cringle, with a shake of her head. "It's no good me saying anything, because directly my back's turned he has his own way again."

The mate shook his head despondently.

"You'd better get your bedding up and make your arrangements forward," said the new skipper presently. There was a look of indulgent admiration in the mate's eye, and she thought it necessary to check it.

"All right," said the other, "plenty of time for that; the river's a little bit thick just now."

"What do you mean?" inquired the girl hastily.

"Some o' these things are not so careful as they might be," said the mate, noting the ominous sparkle of her eye, "an' they might scrape the paint off."

"Look here, my lad," said the new skipper grimly, "if you think you can steer better than me, you'd better keep it to yourself, that's all. Now suppose you see about your bedding, as I said."

The mate went, albeit he was rather surprised at himself for doing so, and hid his annoyance and confusion beneath the mattress which he brought up on his head. His job completed, he came aft again, and, sitting on the hatches, lit his pipe.

"This is just the weather for a pleasant cruise," he said amiably, after a few whiffs. "You've chose a nice time for it."

"I don't mind the weather," said the girl, who fancied that there was a little latent sarcasm somewhere. "I think you'd better wash the decks now."

"Washed 'em last night," said the mate, without moving.

"Ah, after dark, perhaps," said the girl. "Well, I think I'll have them done again."

The mate sat pondering rebelliously for a few minutes, then he removed his jacket, put on in honour of the new skipper, and, fetching the bucket and mop, silently obeyed orders.

"You seem to be very fond of sitting down," remarked the girl, after he had finished; "can't you find something else to do?"

"I don't know," replied the mate slowly; "I thought you were looking after that."

The girl bit her lip, and was looking carefully round her, when they were both disturbed by the unseemly behaviour of the master of a passing craft.

"Jack!" he yelled in a tone of strong amazement, "Jack!"

"Halloa!" cried the mate.

"Why didn't you tell us?" yelled the other reproachfully.

"Tell you what?" roared the mystified mate.

The master of the other craft, holding on to the stays with one hand, jerked his thumb expressively towards Miss Cringle, and waited.

"When was it?" he screamed anxiously, as he realised that his craft was rapidly carrying him out of earshot.

The mate smiled feebly, and glanced uneasily at the girl, who, with a fine colour and an air of vast unconcern, was looking straight in front of her; and it was a relief to both of them when they found themselves hesitating and dodging in front of a schooner which was coming up.

"Do you want all the river?" demanded the exasperated master of the latter vessel, running to the side as they passed. "Why don't you drop anchor if you want to spoon?"

"Perhaps you 'd better let me take the wheel a bit," said the mate, not without a little malice in his voice.

"No; you can go an' keep a look-out in the bows," said the girl serenely. "It'll prevent misunderstandings, too. Better take the potatoes with you and peel them for dinner."

The mate complied, and the voyage proceeded in silence, the steering being rendered a little nicer than usual by various nautical sparks bringing their boats a bit closer than was necessary in order to obtain a good view of the fair steersman.

After dinner, the tide having turned and a stiff head-wind blowing, they brought up off Sheppey. It began to rain hard, and the crew of the Osprey, having made all snug above, retired to the cabin to resume their quarrel.

"Don't mind me," said Miss Cringle scathingly, as the mate lit his pipe.

"Well, I didn't think you minded," replied the mate; "the old man"—

"Who?" interrupted Miss Cringle, in a tone of polite inquiry.

"Captain Cringle," said the mate, correcting himself, "smokes a great deal, and I've heard him say that you liked the smell of it,"

"There's pipes and pipes," said Miss Cringle oracularly.

The mate flung his on the floor and crunched it beneath his heel, then he thrust his hands in his pockets, and, leaning back, scowled darkly up at the rain as it crackled on the skylight.

"If you are going to show off your nasty temper," said the girl severely, "you'd better go forward. It's not quite the thing after all for you to be down here—not that I study appearances much."

"I shouldn't think you did," retorted the mate, whose temper was rapidly getting the better of him. "I can't think what your father was thinking of to let a pret—to let a girl like you come away like this."

"If you were going to say pretty girl," said Miss Cringle, with calm self-abnegation, "don't mind me, say it. The captain knows what he's about. He told me you were a milksop; he said you were a good young man and a teetotaller."

The mate, allowing the truth of the captain's statement as to his abstinence, hotly denied the charge of goodness. "I can understand your father's hurry to get rid of you for a spell," he concluded, being goaded beyond all consideration of politeness. "His gout 'ud never get well while you were with him. More than that, I shouldn't wonder if you were the cause of it."

With this parting shot he departed, before the girl could think of a suitable reply, and went and sulked in the dingy little fo'c'sle.

In the evening, the weather having moderated somewhat, and the tide being on the ebb, they got under way again, the girl coming on deck fully attired in an oilskin coat and sou'-wester to resume the command.

The rain fell steadily as they ploughed along their way, guided by the bright eye of the "Mouse" as it shone across the darkening waters. The mate, soaked to the skin, was at the wheel.

"Why don't you go below and put your oilskins on?" inquired the girl, when this fact dawned upon her.

"Don't want 'em," said the mate.

"I suppose you know best," said the girl, and said no more until nine o'clock, when she paused at the companion to give her last orders for the night.

"I'm going to turn in," said she; "call me at two o'clock. Good-night."

"Good-night," said the other, and the girl vanished.

Left to himself, the mate, who began to feel chilly, felt in his pockets for a pipe, and was in all the stress of getting a light, when he heard a thin, almost mild voice behind him, and, looking round, saw the face of the girl at the companion.

"I say, are these your oilskins I've been wearing?" she demanded awkwardly.

"You're quite welcome," said the mate.

"Why didn't you tell me?" said the girl indignantly. "I wouldn't have worn them for anything if I had known it."

"Well, they won't poison you," said the mate resentfully. "Your father left his at Ipswich to have 'em cobbled up a bit."

The girl passed them up on the deck, and, closing the companion with a bang, disappeared. It is possible that the fatigues of the day had been too much for her, for when she awoke, and consulted the little silver watch that hung by her bunk, it was past five o'clock, and the red glow of the sun was flooding the cabin as she arose and hastily dressed.

The deck was drying in white patches as she went above, and the mate was sitting yawning at the wheel, his eyelids red for want of sleep.

"Didn't I tell you to call me at two o'clock?" she demanded, confronting him.

"It's all right," said the mate. "I thought when you woke would be soon enough. You looked tired."

"I think you'd better go when we get to Ipswich," said the girl, tightening her lips. "I'll ship somebody who'll obey orders."

"I'll go when we get back to London," said the mate. "I'll hand this barge over to the cap'n, and nobody else."

"Well, we'll see," said the girl, as she took the wheel, "I think you'll go at Ipswich."

For the remainder of the voyage the subject was not alluded to; the mate, in a spirit of sulky pride, kept to the fore part of the boat, except when he was steering, and, as far as practicable, the girl ignored his presence. In this spirit of mutual forbearance they entered the Orwell, and ran swiftly up to Ipswich.

It was late in the afternoon when they arrived there, and the new skipper, waiting only until they were made fast, went ashore, leaving the mate in charge. She had been gone about an hour when a small telegraph boy appeared, and, after boarding the barge in the unsafest manner possible, handed him a telegram. The mate read it and his face flushed. With even more than the curtness customary in language at a halfpenny a word, it contained his dismissal.

"I've had a telegram from your father sacking me," he said to the girl, as she returned soon after, laden with small parcels.

"Yes, I wired him to," she replied calmly. "I suppose you'll go NOW?"

"I'd rather go back to London with you," he said slowly.

"I daresay," said the girl. "As a matter of fact I wasn't really meaning for you to go, but when you said you wouldn't I thought we'd see who was master. I've shipped another mate, so you see I haven't lost much time."

"Who is he," inquired the mate.

"Man named Charlie Lee," replied the girl; "the foreman here told me of him."

"He'd no business too," said the mate, frowning; "he's a loose fish; take my advice now and ship somebody else. He's not at all the sort of chap I'd choose for you to sail with."

"You'd choose," said the girl scornfully; "dear me, what a pity you didn't tell me before."

"He's a public-house loafer," said the mate, meeting her eye angrily, "and about as bad as they make 'em; but I s'pose you'll have your own way."

"He won't frighten me," said the girl. "I'm quite capable of taking care of myself, thank you. Good evening."

The mate stepped ashore with a small bundle, leaving the remainder of his possessions to go back to London with the barge. The girl watched his well-knit figure as it strode up the quay until it was out of sight, and then, inwardly piqued because he had not turned round for a parting glance, gave a little sigh, and went below to tea.

The docile and respectful behaviour of the new-comer was a pleasant change to the autocrat of the Osprey, and cargoes were worked out and in without an unpleasant word. They laid at the quay for two days, the new mate, whose home was at Ipswich, sleeping ashore, and on the morning of the third he turned up punctually at six o'clock, and they started on their return voyage.

"Well, you do know how to handle a craft," said Lee admiringly, as they passed down the river. "The old boat seems to know it's got a pretty young lady in charge."

"Don't talk rubbish," said the girl austerely.

The new mate carefully adjusted his red necktie and smiled indulgently.

"Well, you're the prettiest cap'n I've ever sailed under," he said. "What do they call that red cap you've got on? Tam-o'-Shanter is it?"

"I don't know," said the girl shortly.

"You mean you won't tell me," said the other, with a look of anger in his soft dark eyes.

"Just as you like," said she, and Lee, whistling softly, turned on his heel and began to busy himself with some small matter forward.

The rest of the day passed quietly, though there was a freedom in the new mate's manner which made the redoubtable skipper of the Osprey regret her change of crew, and to treat him with more civility than her proud spirit quite approved of. There was but little wind, and the barge merely crawled along as the captain and mate, with surreptitious glances, took each other's measure.

"This is the nicest trip I've ever had," said Lee, as he came up from an unduly prolonged tea, with a strong-smelling cigar in his mouth. "I've brought your jacket up."

"I don't want it, thank you," said the girl.

"Better have it," said Lee, holding it up for her.

"When I want my jacket I'll put it on myself," said the girl.

"All right, no offence," said the other airily. "What an obstinate little devil you are."

"Have you got any drink down there?" inquired the girl, eyeing him sternly.

"Just a little drop o' whiskey, my dear, for the spasms," said Lee facetiously. "Will you have a drop?"

"I won't have any drinking here," said she sharply. "If you want to drink, wait till you get ashore."

"YOU won't have any drinking!" said the other, opening his eyes, and with a quiet chuckle he dived below and brought up a bottle and a glass. "Here's wishing a better temper to you, my dear," he said amiably, as he tossed off a glass. "Come, you'd better have a drop. It'll put a little colour in your cheeks."

"Put it away now, there's a good fellow," said the captain timidly, as she looked anxiously at the nearest sail, some two miles distant.

"It's the only friend I've got," said Lee, sprawling gracefully on the hatches, and replenishing his glass. "Look here. Are you on for a bargain?"

"What do you mean?" inquired the girl.

"Give me a kiss, little spitfire, and I won't take another drop to-night," said the new mate tenderly. "Come, I won't tell."

"You may drink yourself to death before I'll do that," said the girl, striving to speak calmly. "Don't talk that nonsense to me again."

She stooped over as she spoke and made a sudden grab at the bottle, but the new mate was too quick for her, and, snatching it up jeeringly, dared her to come for it.

"Come on, come and fight for it," said he; "hit me if you like, I don't mind; your little fist won't hurt."

No answer being vouchsafed to this invitation he applied himself to his only friend again, while the girl, now thoroughly frightened, steered in silence.

"Better get the sidelights out," said she at length.

"Plenty o' time," said Lee.

"Take the helm, then, while I do it," said the girl, biting her lips.

The fellow rose and came towards her, and, as she made way for him, threw his arm round her waist and tried to detain her. Her heart beating quickly, she walked forward, and, not without a hesitating glance at the drunken figure at the wheel, descended into the fo'c'sle for the lamps.

The next moment, with a gasping little cry, she sank down on a locker as the dark figure of a man rose and stood by her.

"Don't be frightened," it said quietly.

"Jack?" said the girl.

"That's me," said the figure. "You didn't expect to see me, did you? I thought perhaps you didn't know what was good for you, so I stowed myself away last night, and here I am."

"Have you heard what that fellow has been saying to me?" demanded Miss Cringle, with a spice of the old temper leavening her voice once more.

"Every word," said the mate cheerfully.

"Why didn't you come up and stand by me?" inquired the girl hotly.

The mate hung his head.

"Oh," said the girl, and her tones were those of acute disappointment, "you're afraid."

"I'm not," said the mate scornfully.

"Why didn't you come up, then, instead of skulking down here?" inquired the girl.

"The mate scratched the back of his neck and smiled, but weakly. "Well, I—I thought"—he began, and stopped.

"You thought"—prompted Miss Cringle coldly.

"I thought a little fright would do you good," said the mate, speaking quickly, "and that it would make you appreciate me a little more when I did come."

"Ahoy! MAGGIE! MAGGIE!" came the voice of the graceless varlet who was steering.

"I'll MAGGIE him," said the mate, grinding his teeth, "Why, what the—why you 're crying."

"I'm not," sobbed Miss Cringle scornfully. "I'm in a temper, that's all."

"I'll knock his head off," said the mate; "you stay down here."

"Mag-GIE!" came the voice again, "MAG—HULLO!"

"Were you calling me, my lad?" said the mate, with dangerous politeness, as he stepped aft. "Ain't you afraid of straining that sweet voice o' yours? Leave go o' that tiller."

The other let go, and the mate's fist took him heavily in the face and sent him sprawling on the deck. He rose with a scream of rage and rushed at his opponent, but the mate's temper, which had suffered badly through his treatment of the last few days, was up, and he sent him heavily down again.

"There's a little dark dingy hole forward," said the mate, after waiting some time for him to rise again, "just the place for you to go and think over your sins in. If I see you come out of it until we get to London, I'll hurt you. Now clear."

The other cleared, and, carefully avoiding the girl, who was standing close by, disappeared below.

"You've hurt him," said the girl, coming up to the mate and laying her hand on his arm. "What a horrid temper you've got."

"It was him asking you to kiss him that upset me," said the mate apologetically.

"He put his arm round my waist," said Miss Cringle, blushing.

"WHAT!" said the mate, stuttering, "put his—put his arm—round—your waist—like"—

His courage suddenly forsook him.

"Like what?" inquired the girl, with superb innocence.

"Like THAT," said the mate manfully.

"That'll do," said Miss Cringle softly, "that'll do. You're as bad as he is, only the worst of it is there is nobody here to prevent you."

SMOKED SKIPPER

Wapping Old Stairs?" said the rough individual, shouldering the bran-new sea-chest, and starting off at a trot with it; "yus, I know the place, captin. Fust v'y'ge, sir?"

"Ay, ay, my hearty," replied the owner of the chest, a small, ill-looking lad of fourteen. "Not so fast with those timbers of yours. D'ye hear?"

"All right, sir," said the man, and, slackening his pace, twisted his head round to take stock of his companion.

"This ain't your fust v'y'ge, captin," he said admiringly; "don't tell me. I could twig that directly I see you. Ho, what's the use o' trying to come it over a poor 'ard-working man like that?"

"I don't think there's much about the sea I don't know," said the boy in a satisfied voice. "Starboard, starboard your hellum a bit."

The man obeying promptly, they went the remainder of the distance in this fashion, to the great inconvenience of people coming from the other direction.

"And a cheap 'arf-crown's worth, too, captin," said the man, as he put the chest down at the head of the stairs and thoughtfully sat on it pending payment.

"I want to go off to the Susan Jane," said the boy, turning to a waterman who was sitting in his boat, holding on to the side of the steps with his hand.

"All right," said the man, "give us a hold o' your box."

"Put it aboard," said the boy to the other man.

"A' right, captin," said the man, with a cheerful smile, "but I'll 'ave my 'arf-crown fust if you don't mind."

"But you said sixpence at the station," said the boy.

"Two an' sixpence, captin," said the man, still smiling, "but I'm a bit 'usky, an' p'raps you didn't hear the two—'arf a crown's the regler price. We ain't allowed to do it under."

"Well, I won't tell anybody," said the boy.

"Give the man 'is 'arf-crown," said the waterman, with sudden heat; "that's 'is price, and my fare's eigh-teen pence."

"All right," said the boy readily; "cheap, too. I didn't know the price, that's all. But I can't pay either of you till I get aboard. I've only got sixpence. I'll tell the captain to give you the rest."

"Tell 'oo?" demanded the light-porter, with some violence.

"The captain," said the boy.

"Look 'ere, you give me that 'arf-crown," said the other, "else I'll chuck your box overboard, an' you after it."

"Wait a minute, then," said the boy, darting away up the narrow alley which led to the stairs; "I'll go and get change."

"'E's goin' to change 'arf a suvren, or p'raps a suvren," said the waterman; "you'd better make it five bob, matey."

"Ah, an' you make yours more," said the light-porter cordially. "Well, I'm— Well of all the—"

"Get off that box," said the big policeman who had come back with the boy. "Take your sixpence an' go. If I catch you down this way again—"

He finished the sentence by taking the fellow by the scruff of the neck and giving him a violent push as he passed him.

"Waterman's fare is threepence," he said to the boy, as the man in the boat, with an utterly expressionless face, took the chest from him, "I'll stay here till he has put you aboard."

The boy took his seat, and the waterman, breathing hard, pulled out towards the vessels in the tier. He looked at the boy and then at the figure on the steps, and, apparently suppressing a strong inclination to speak, spat violently over the side.

"Fine big chap, ain't he?" said the boy.

The waterman, affecting not to hear, looked over his shoulder, and pulled strongly with his left towards a small schooner, from the deck of which a couple of men were watching the small figure in the boat.

"That's the boy I was going to tell you about," said the skipper, "and remember this 'ere ship's a pirate."

"It's got a lot o' pirates aboard of it," said the mate fiercely, as he turned and regarded the crew, "a set o' lazy, loafing, idle, worthless—"

"It's for the boy's sake," interrupted the skipper.

"Where'd you pick him up?" inquired the other.

"He's the son of a friend o' mine what I've brought aboard to oblige," replied the skipper. "He's got a fancy for being a pirate, so just to oblige his father I told him we was a pirate. He wouldn't have come if I hadn't."

"I'll pirate him," said the mate, rubbing his hands.

"He's a dreadful 'andful, by all accounts," continued the other; "got his 'ed stuffed full o' these 'ere penny dreadfuls till they've turned his brain almost. He started by being an Indian, and goin' off on 'is own with two other kids. When 'e wanted to turn cannibal the other two objected, and gave 'im in charge. After that he did a bit o' burgling, and it cost 'is old man no end o' money to hush it up."

"Well, what did you want him for?" grumbled the mate.

"I'm goin' to knock the nonsense out of him," said the skipper softly, as the boat grazed the side. "Just step for'ard and let the hands know what's expected of 'em. When we get to sea it won't matter."

The mate moved off grumbling, as the small fare stood on the thwarts and scrambled up over the side. The waterman passed up the chest, and dropping the coppers into his pocket, pushed off again without a word.

"Well, you've got here all right, Ralph?" said the skipper. "What do you think of her?"

"She's a rakish-looking craft," said the boy, looking round the dingy old tub with much satisfaction; "but where's your arms?"

"Hush!" said the skipper, and laid his finger on his nose.

"Oh, all right," said the youth testily, "but you might tell me."

"You shall know all in good time," said the skipper patiently, turning to the crew, who came shuffling up, masking broad grins with dirty palms.

"Here's a new shipmate for you, my lads. He's small, but he's the right stuff."

The newcomer drew himself up, and regarded the crew with some dissatisfaction. For desperadoes they looked far too good-tempered and prone to levity.

"What's the matter with you, Jem Smithers?" inquired the skipper, scowling at a huge fair-haired man, who was laughing discordantly.

"I was thinkin' o' the last party I killed, sir," said Jem, with sudden gravity. "I allers laugh when I think 'ow he squealed."

"You laugh too much," said the other sternly, as he laid a hand on Ralph's shoulder. "Take a lesson from this fine feller; he don't laugh. He acts. Take 'im down below an' show him 'is bunk."

"Will you please to follow me, sir?" said Smithers, leading the way below. "I dessay you'll find it a bit stuffy, but that's owing to Bill Dobbs. A regler old sea-dog is Bill, always sleeps in 'is clothes and never washes."

"I don't think the worse of him for that," said Ralph, regarding the fermenting Dobbs kindly.

"You'd best keep a civil tongue in your 'ed, my lad," said Dobbs shortly.

"Never mind 'im," said Smithers cheerfully; "nobody takes any notice o' old Dobbs. You can 'it 'im if you like. I won't let him hurt you."

"I don't want to start by quarrelling," said Ralph seriously.

"You're afraid," said Jem tauntingly; "you'll never make one of us. 'It 'im; I won't let him hurt you."

Thus aroused, the boy, first directing Dobbs' attention to his stomach by a curious duck of the head, much admired as a feint in his neighbourhood, struck him in the face. The next moment the forecastle was in an uproar and Ralph prostrate on Dobbs' knees, frantically reminding Jem of his promise.

"All right, I won't let him 'urt you," said Jem consolingly.

"But he is hurting me," yelled the boy. "He's hurting me now."

"Well, wait till I get 'im ashore," said Jem, "his old woman won't know him when I've done with him."

The boy's reply to this was a torrent of shrill abuse, principally directed to Jem's facial shortcomings.

"Now don't get rude," said the seaman, grinning.

"Squint-eyes," cried Ralph fiercely.

"When you've done with that 'ere young gentleman, Dobbs," said Jem, with exquisite politeness, "I should like to 'ave 'im for a little bit to teach 'im manners."

"'E don't want to go," said Dobbs, grinning, as Ralph clung to him. "He knows who's kind to him."

"Wait till I get a chance at you," sobbed Ralph, as Jem took him away from Dobbs.

"Lord lumme," said Jem, regarding him in astonishment. "Why, he's actooaly cryin'. I've seen a good many pirates in my time, Bill, but this is a new sort."

"Leave the boy alone," said the cook, a fat, good-natured man. "Here, come 'ere, old man. They don't mean no 'arm."

Glad to escape, Ralph made his way over to the cook, grinding his teeth with shame as that worthy took him between his knees and mopped his eyes with something which he called a handkerchief.

"You'll be all right," he said kindly. "You'll be as good a pirate as any of us before you've finished."

"Wait till the first engagement, that's all," sobbed the boy. "If somebody don't get shot in the back it won't be my fault."

The two seamen looked at each other. "That's wot hurt my 'and then," said Dobbs slowly. "I thought it was a jack-knife."

He reached over, and unceremoniously grabbing the boy by the collar, pulled him towards him, and drew a small cheap revolver from his pocket. "Look at that, Jem."

"Take your fingers orf the blessed trigger and then I will," said the other, somewhat sourly.

"I'll pitch it overboard," said Dobbs.

"Don't be a fool, Bill," said Smithers, pocketing it, "that's worth a few pints o' anybody's money. Stand out o' the way, Bill, the Pirit King wants to go on deck."

Bill moved aside as the boy went to the ladder, and allowing him to get up four or five steps, did the rest for him with his shoulder. The boy reached the deck on all fours, and, regaining a more dignified position as soon as possible, went and leaned over the side, regarding with lofty contempt the busy drudges on wharf and river.

They sailed at midnight and brought up in the early dawn in Longreach, where a lighter loaded with barrels came alongside, and the boy smelt romance and mystery when he learnt that they contained powder. They took in ten tons, the lighter drifted away, the hatches were put on, and they started once more.

It was his first voyage, and he regarded with eager interest the craft passing up and down. He had made his peace with the seamen, and they regaled him with blood-curdling stories of their adventures, in the vain hope of horrifying him.

"'E's a beastly little rascal, that's wot 'e is," said the indignant Bill, who had surprised himself by his powers of narration; "fancy larfin' when I told 'im of pitchin' the baby to the sharks."

"'E's all right, Bill," said the cook softly. "Wait till you've got seven of 'em."

"What are you doing here, boy?" demanded the skipper, as Ralph, finding the seamen's yarns somewhat lacking in interest, strolled aft with his hands in his pockets.

"Nothing," said the boy, staring.

"Keep the other end o' the ship," said the skipper sharply, "an' go an' 'elp the cook with the taters."

Ralph hesitated, but a grin on the mate's face decided him.

"I didn't come here to peel potatoes," he said loftily.

"Oh, indeed," said the skipper politely; "an' wot might you 'ave come for, if it ain't being too inquisitive?"

"To fight the enemy," said Ralph shortly.

"Come 'ere," said the skipper.

The boy came slowly towards him.

"Now look 'ere," said the skipper, "I'm going to try and knock a little sense into that stupid 'ed o' yours. I've 'eard all about your silly little games ashore. Your father said he couldn't manage you, so I'm goin' to have a try, and you'll find I'm a very different sort o' man to deal with to wot 'e is. The idea o' thinking this ship was a pirate. Why, a boy your age ought to know there ain't such things nowadays."

"You told me you was," said the boy hotly, "else I wouldn't have come."

"That's just why I told you," said the skipper. "But I didn't think you'd be such a fool as to believe it. Pirates, indeed! Do we look like pirates?"

"You don't," said the boy with a sneer; "you look more like—"

"Like wot?" asked the skipper, edging closer to him. "Eh, like wot?"

"I forget the word," said Ralph, with strong good sense.

"Don't tell any lies now," said the skipper, flushing, as he heard a chuckle from the mate. "Go on, out with it. I'll give you just two minutes."

"I forget it," persisted Ralph.

"Dustman?" suggested the mate, coming to his assistance. "Coster, chimbley-sweep, mudlark, pickpocket, convict, washer-worn—"

"If you'll look after your dooty, George, instead o' interferin' in matters that don't concern you," said the skipper in a choking voice, "I shall be obliged. Now, then, you boy, what were you going to say I was like?"

"Like the mate," said Ralph slowly.

"Don't tell lies," said the skipper furiously; "you couldn't 'ave forgot that word."

"I didn't forget it," said Ralph, "but I didn't know how you'd like it."

The skipper looked at him dubiously, and pushing his cap from his brow scratched his head.

"And I didn't know how the mate 'ud like it, either," continued the boy.

He relieved the skipper from an awkward dilemma by walking off to the galley and starting on a bowl of potatoes. The master of the Susan Jane watched him blankly for some time and then looked round at the mate.

"You won't get much change out of 'im," said the latter, with a nod; "insultin' little devil."

The other made no reply, but as soon as the potatoes were finished set his young friend to clean brass work, and after that to tidy the cabin up and help the cook clean his pots and pans. Meantime the mate went below and overhauled his chest.

"This is where he gets all them ideas from," he said, coming aft with a big bundle of penny papers. "Look at the titles of 'em—'The Lion of the Pacific,' 'The One-armed Buccaneer,' 'Captain Kidd's Last Voyage.'"

He sat down on the cabin skylight and began turning them over, and, picking out certain gems of phraseology, read them aloud to the skipper. The latter listened at first with scorn and then with impatience.

"I can't make head or tail out of what you're reading, George," he said snappishly. "Who was Rudolph? Read straight ahead."

Thus urged, the mate, leaning forward so that his listener might hear better, read steadily through a serial in the first three numbers. The third instalment left Rudolph swimming in a race with three sharks and a boat-load of cannibals; and the joint efforts of both men failed to discover the other numbers.

"Just wot I should 'ave expected of 'im," said the skipper, as the mate returned from a fruitless search in the boy's chest. "I'll make him a bit more orderly on this ship. Go an' lock them other things up in your drawer, George. He's not to 'ave 'em again."

The schooner was getting into open water now, and began to feel it. In front of them was the blue sea, dotted with white sails and funnels belching smoke, speeding from England to worlds of romance and adventure. Something of the kind the cook said to Ralph, and urged him to get up and look for himself. He also, with the best intentions, discussed the restorative properties of fat pork from a medical point of view.

The next few days the boy divided between seasickness and work, the latter being the skipper's great remedy for piratical yearnings. Three or four times he received a mild drubbing, and, what was worse than the drubbing, had to give an answer in the affirmative to the skipper's inquiry as to whether he felt in a more wholesome frame of mind. On the fifth morning they stood in towards Fairhaven, and to his great joy he saw trees and houses again.

They stayed at Fairhaven just long enough to put out a small portion of their cargo, Ralph, stripped to his shirt and trousers, having to work in the hold with the rest, and proceeded to Lowport, a little place some thirty miles distant, to put out their powder.

It was evening before they arrived, and, the tide being out, anchored in the mouth of the river on which the town stands.

"Git in about four o'clock," said the skipper to the mate, as he looked over the side towards the little cluster of houses on the shore. "Do you feel better now I've knocked some o' that nonsense out o' you, boy?"

"Much better, sir," said Ralph respectfully.

"Be a good boy," said the skipper, pausing on the companion-ladder, "and you can stay with us if you like. Better turn in now, as you'll have to make yourself useful again in the morning working out the cargo."

He went below, leaving the boy on deck. The crew were in the forecastle smoking, with the exception of the cook, who was in the galley over a little private business of his own.

An hour later the cook went below to prepare for sleep. The other two men were already in bed, and he was about to get into his when he noticed that Ralph's bunk, which was under his own, was empty. He went up on deck and looked round, and, returning below, scratched his nose in thought.

"Where's the boy?" he demanded, taking Jem by the arm and shaking him.

"Eh?" said Jem, rousing. "Whose boy?"

"Our boy, Ralph," said the cook. "I can't see 'im nowhere. I 'ope 'e ain't gone overboard, pore little chap."

Jem refusing to discuss the matter, the cook awoke Dobbs. Dobbs swore at him peacefully, and resumed his slumbers. The cook went up again and prowled round the deck, looking in all sorts of unlikely places for the boy. He even climbed a little way into the rigging, and, finding no traces of him, was reluctantly forced to the conclusion that he had gone overboard.

"Pore little chap," he said solemnly, looking over the ship's side at the still water.

He walked slowly aft, shaking his head, and looking over the stern, brought up suddenly with a cry of dismay and rubbed his eyes. The ship's boat had also disappeared.

"Wot?" said the two seamen as he ran below and communicated the news. "Well, if it's gorn, it's gorn."

"Hadn't I better go an' tell the skipper?" said the cook.

"Let 'im find it out 'isself," said Jem, purring contentedly in the blankets. "It's 'is boat. Go' night."

"Time we 'ad a noo 'un too," said Dobbs, yawning. "Don't you worry your 'ed, cook, about what don't consarn you."

The cook took the advice, and, having made his few simple preparations for the night, blew out the lamp and sprang into his bunk. Then he uttered a sharp exclamation, and getting out again fumbled for the matches and relit the lamp. A minute later he awoke his exasperated friends for the third time.

"S'elp me, cook," began Jem fiercely.

"If you don't I will," said Dobbs, sitting up and trying to reach the cook with his clenched fist.

"It's a letter pinned to my pillow," said the cook in trembling tones, as he held it to the lamp.

"Well, we don't want to 'ear it," said Jem. "Shut up, d'ye hear?"

But there was that in the cook's manner which awed him.

"Dear cook," he read feverishly, "I have made an infernal machine with clockwork, and hid it in the hold near the gunpowder when we were at Fairhaven. I think it will go off between ten and eleven to-night, but I am not quite sure about the time. Don't tell those other beasts, but jump overboard and swim ashore. I have taken the boat I would have taken you too, but you told me you swam seven miles once, so you can eas—"

The reading came to an abrupt termination as his listeners sprang out of their bunks, and, bolting on dock, burst wildly into the cabin, and breathlessly reeled off the heads of the letter to its astonished occupants.

"Stuck a wot in the hold?" gasped the skipper.

"Infernal machine," said the mate; "one of them things wot you blow up the 'Ouses of Parliament with."

"Wot's the time now?" interrogated Jem anxiously.

"'Bout ha'-past ten," said the cook trembling. "Let's give 'em a hail ashore."

They leaned over the side, and sent a mighty shout across the water. Most of Lowport had gone to bed, but the windows in the inn were bright, and lights showed in the upper windows of two or three of the cottages.

Again they shouted in deafening chorus, casting fearful looks behind them, and in the silence a faint answering hail came from the shore. They shouted again like madmen, until listening intently they heard a boat's keel grate on the beach, and then the welcome click of oars in the rowlocks.

"Make haste," bawled Dobbs vociferously, as the boat came creeping out of the darkness. "W'y don't you make 'aste?"

"Wot's the row?" cried a voice from the boat.

"Gunpowder!" yelled the cook frantically; "there's ten tons of it aboard just going to explode. Hurry up."

The sound of the oars ceased and a startled murmur was heard from the boat; then an oar was pulled jerkily.

"They're putting back," said Jem suddenly. "I'm going to swim for it. Stand by to pick me up, mates," he shouted, and lowering himself with a splash into the water struck out strongly towards them.

Dobbs, a poor swimmer, after a moment's hesitation, followed his example.

"I can't swim a stroke," cried the cook, his teeth chattering.

The others, who were in the same predicament, leaned over the side, listening. The swimmers were invisible in the darkness, but their progress was easily followed by the noise they made. Jem was the first to be hauled on board, and a minute or two later the listeners on the schooner heard him assisting Dobbs. Then the sounds of strife, of thumps, and wicked words broke on their delighted ears.

"They're coming back for us," said the mate, taking a deep breath. "Well done, Jem."

The boat came towards them, impelled by powerful strokes, and was soon alongside. The three men tumbled in hurriedly, their fall being modified by the original crew, who were lying crouched up in the bottom of the boat. Jem and Dobbs gave way with hearty goodwill, and the doomed ship receded into the darkness. A little knot of people had gathered on the shore, and, receiving the tidings, became anxious for the safety of their town. It was felt that the windows, at least, were in imminent peril, and messengers were hastily sent round to have them opened.

Still the deserted Susan Jane made no sign. Twelve o'clock struck from the little church at the back of the town, and she was still intact.

"Something's gone wrong," said an old fisherman with a bad way of putting things. "Now's the time for somebody to go and tow her out to sea."

There was no response.

"To save Lowport," said the speaker feelingly.. "If I was only twenty years younger—"

"It's old men's work," said a voice.

The skipper, straining his eyes through the gloom in the direction of his craft, said nothing. He began to think that she had escaped after all.

Two o'clock struck, and the crowd began to disperse..Some of the bolder inhabitants who were fidgety about draughts closed their windows, and children who had been routed out of their beds to take a nocturnal walk inland were led slowly back. By three o'clock the danger was felt to be over, and day broke and revealed the forlorn Susan Jane still riding at anchor.

"I'm going aboard," said the skipper suddenly; "who's coming with me?"

Jem and the mate and the town policeman volunteered, and, borrowing the boat which had served them before, pulled swiftly out to their vessel, and, taking the hatches off with unusual gentleness, commenced their search. It was nervous work at first, but they became inured to it, and, moreover, a certain suspicion, slight at first, but increasing in intensity as the search proceeded, gave them some sense of security. Later still they began to eye each other shamefacedly.

"I don't believe there's anything there," said the policeman, sitting down and laughing boisterously; "that boy's been making a fool of you."

"That's about the size of it," groaned the mate. "We'll be the laughing-stock o' the town."

The skipper, who was standing with his back towards him, said nothing; but, peering about, stooped suddenly, and, with a sharp exclamation, picked up something from behind a damaged case.

"I've got it," he yelled suddenly; "stand clear!"

He scrambled hastily on deck, and, holding his find at arm's length, with his head averted, flung it far into the water. A loud cheer from a couple of boats which were watching greeted his action, and a distant response came from the shore.

"Was that a infernal machine?" whispered the bewildered Jem to the mate. "Why, it looked to me just like one o' them tins o' corned beef."

The mate shook his head at him and glanced at the constable, who was gazing longingly over the side. "Well, I've 'eard of people being killed by them sometimes," he said with a grin.

STEPPING BACKWARDS

"Wonderful improvement," said Mr. Jack Mills. "Show 'em to me again."

Mr. Simpson took his pipe from his mouth and, parting his lips, revealed his new teeth.

"And you talk better," said Mr. Mills, taking his glass from the counter and emptying it; "you ain't got that silly lisp you used to have. What does your missis think of 'em?"

"She hasn't seen 'em yet," said the other. "I had 'em put in at dinner-time. I ate my dinner with 'em."

Mr. Mills expressed his admiration. "If it wasn't for your white hair and whiskers you'd look thirty again," he said, slowly. "How old are you?"

"Fifty-three," said his friend. "If it wasn't for being laughed at I've often thought of having my whiskers shaved off and my hair dyed black. People think I'm sixty."

"Or seventy," continued Mr. Mills. "What does it matter, people laughing? You've got a splendid head of 'air, and it would dye beautiful."

Mr. Simpson shook his head and, ordering a couple of glasses of bitter, attacked his in silence.

"It might be done gradual," he said, after a long interval. "It don't do anybody good at the warehouse to look old."

"Make a clean job of it," counselled Mr. Mills, who was very fond of a little cheap excitement. "Get it over and done with. You've got good features, and you'd look splendid clean-shaved." Mr. Simpson smiled faintly. "Only on Wednesday the barmaid here was asking after you," pursued Mr. Mills. Mr. Simpson smiled again. "She says to me, 'Where's Gran'pa?' she says, and when I says, haughty like, 'Who do you mean?' she says, 'Father Christmas!' If you was to tell her that you are only fifty-three, she'd laugh in your face."

"Let her laugh," said the other, sourly.

"Come out and get it off," said Mr. Mills, earnestly. "There's a barber's in Bird Street; you could go in the little back room, where he charges a penny more, and get it done without anybody being a bit the wiser."

He put his hand on Mr. Simpson's shoulder, and that gentleman, with a glare in the direction of the fair but unconscious offender, rose in a hypnotized fashion and followed him out. Twice on the way to Bird Street Mr. Simpson paused and said he had altered his mind, and twice did the propulsion of Mr. Mills's right hand, and his flattering argument, make him alter it again.

It was a matter of relief to Mr. Simpson that the barber took his instructions without any show of surprise. It appeared, indeed, that an elderly man of seventy-eight had enlisted his services for a similar purpose not two months before, and had got married six weeks afterwards. Age of the bride given as twenty-four, but said to have looked older.

A snip of the scissors, and six inches of white beard fell to the floor. For the first time in thirty years Mr. Simpson felt a razor on his face. Then his hair was cut and shampooed; and an hour later he sat gazing at a dark-haired, clean-shaven man in the glass who gazed back at him with wondering eyes— a lean-jawed, good-looking man, who, in a favourable light, might pass for forty. He turned and met the admiring eyes of Mr. Mills.

"What did I tell you?" inquired the latter. "You look young enough to be your own son."

"Or grandson," said the barber, with professional pride.

Mr. Simpson got up slowly from the chair and, accompanied by the admiring Mr. Mills, passed out into the street. The evening was young, and, at his friend's suggestion, they returned to the Plume of Feathers.

"You give the order," said Mr. Mills, "and see whether she recognizes you."

Mr. Simpson obeyed.

"Don't you know him?" inquired Mr. Mills, as the barmaid turned away.

"I don't think I have that pleasure," said the girl, simpering.

"Gran'pa's eldest boy," said Mr. Mills.

"Oh!" said the girl. "Well, I hope he's a better man than his father, then?"

"What do you mean by that?" demanded Mr. Simpson, painfully conscious of his friend's regards.

"Nothing," said the girl, "nothing. Only we can all be better, can't we? He's a nice old gentleman; so simple."

"Don't know you from Adam," said Mr. Mills, as she turned away. "Now, if you ask me, I don't believe as your own missis will recognize you."

"Rubbish," said Mr. Simpson. "My wife would know me anywhere. We've been married over thirty years. Thirty years of sunshine and shadow together. You're a single man, and don't understand these things."

"P'r'aps you're right," said his friend. "But it'll be a bit of a shock to her, anyway. What do you say to me stepping round and breaking the news to her? It's a bit sudden, you know. She's expecting a white-haired old gentleman, not a black-haired boy."

Mr. Simpson looked a bit uneasy. "P'r'aps I ought to have told her first," he murmured, craning his neck to look in the glass at the back of the bar.

"I'll go and put it right for you," said his friend. "You stay here and smoke your pipe."

He stepped out briskly, but his pace slackened as he drew near the house.

"I—I—came—to see you about your husband," he faltered, as Mrs. Simpson opened the door and stood regarding him.

"What's the matter?" she exclaimed, with a faint cry. "What's happened to him?"

"Nothing," said Mr. Mills, hastily. "Nothing serious, that is. I just came round to warn you so that you will be able to know it's him."

Mrs. Simpson let off a shriek that set his ears tingling. Then, steadying herself by the wall, she tottered into the front room, followed by the discomfited Mr. Mills, and sank into a chair.

"He's dead!" she sobbed. "He's dead!"

"He is not," said Mr. Mills.

"Is he much hurt? Is he dying?" gasped Mrs. Simpson.

"Only his hair," said Mr. Mills, clutching at the opening. "He is not hurt at all."

Mrs. Simpson dabbed at her eyes-and sat regarding him in bewilderment. Her twin chins were still quivering with emotion, but her eyes were beginning to harden. "What are you talking about?" she inquired, in a raspy voice.

"He's been to a hairdresser's," said Mr. Mills. "He's 'ad all his white whiskers cut off, and his hair cut short and dyed black. And, what with that and his new teeth, I thought—he thought—p'r'aps you mightn't know him when he came home."

"Dyed?" cried Mrs. Simpson, starting to her feet.

Mr. Mills nodded. "He looks twenty years younger," he said, with a smile. "He'd pass for his own son anywhere."

Mrs. Simpson's eyes snapped. "Perhaps he'd pass for my son," she remarked.

"Yes, easy," said the tactful Mr. Mills. "You can't think what a difference it's made to him. That's why I came to see you—so you shouldn't be startled."

"Thank you," said Mrs. Simpson. "I'm much obliged. But you might have spared yourself the trouble. I should know my husband anywhere."

"Ah, that's what you think," retorted Mr. Mills, with a smile; "but the barmaid at the Plume didn't. That's what made me come to you."

Mrs. Simpson gazed at him.

"I says to myself," continued Mr. Mills, "'If she don't know him, I'm certain his missis won't, and I'd better—'"

"You'd better go," interrupted his hostess.

Mr. Mills started, and then, with much dignity, stalked after her to the door.

"As to your story, I don't believe a word of it," said Mrs. Simpson. "Whatever else my husband is, he isn't a fool, and he'd no more think of cutting off his whiskers and dyeing his hair than you would of telling the truth."

"Seeing is believing," said the offended Mr. Mills, darkly.

"I'll wait till I do see, and then I sha'n't believe," was the reply. "It is a put-up job between you and some other precious idiot, I expect. But you can't deceive me. If your black-haired friend comes here, he'll get it, I can tell you."

She slammed the door on his protests and, returning to the parlour, gazed fiercely into the glass on the mantelpiece. It reflected sixteen stone of honest English womanhood, a thin wisp of yellowish-grey hair, and a pair of faded eyes peering through clumsy spectacles.

"Son, indeed!" she said, her lips quivering. "You wait till you come home, my lord!"

Mr. Simpson, with some forebodings, returned home an hour later. To a man who loved peace and quietness the report of the indignant Mr. Mills was not of a reassuring nature. He hesitated on the doorstep for a few seconds while he fumbled for his key, and then, humming unconcernedly, hung his hat in the passage and walked into the parlour.

The astonished scream of his wife warned him that Mr. Mills had by no means exaggerated. She rose from her seat and, crouching by the fireplace, regarded him with a mixture of anger and dismay.

"It—it's all right, Milly," said Mr. Simpson, with a smile that revealed a dazzling set of teeth.

"Who are you?" demanded Mrs. Simpson. "How dare you call me by my Christian name. It's a good job for you my husband is not here."

"He wouldn't hurt me," said Mr. Simpson, with an attempt at facetiousness. "He's the best friend I ever had. Why, we slept in the same cradle."

"I don't want any of your nonsense," said Mrs. Simpson. "You get out of my house before I send for the police. How dare you come into a respectable woman's house in this fashion? Be off with you."

"Now, look here, Milly—" began Mr. Simpson.

His wife drew herself up to her full height of four feet eleven.

"I've had a hair-cut and a shave," pursued her husband; "also I've had my hair restored to its natural colour. But I'm the same man, and you know it."

"I know nothing of the kind," said his wife, doggedly. "I don't know you from Adam. I've never seen you before, and I don't want to see you again. You go away."

"I'm your husband, and my place is at home," replied Mr. Simpson. "A man can have a shave if he likes, can't he? Where's my supper?"

"Go on," said his wife. "Keep it up. But be careful my husband don't come in and catch you, that's all."

Mr. Simpson gazed at her fixedly, and then, with an impatient exclamation, walked into the small kitchen and began to set the supper. A joint of cold beef, a jar of pickles, bread, butter, and cheese made an appetizing display. Then he took a jug from the dresser and descended to the cellar.

A musical trickling fell on the ear of Mrs. Simpson as she stood at the parlour door, and drew her stealthily to the cellar. The key was in the lock, and, with a sudden movement, she closed the door and locked it. A sharp cry from Mr. Simpson testified to his discomfiture.

"Now I'm off for the police," cried his wife.

"Don't be a fool," shouted Mr. Simpson, tugging wildly at the door-handle. "Open the door."

Mrs. Simpson remained silent, and her husband resumed his efforts until the door-knob, unused to such treatment, came off in his hand. A sudden scrambling noise on the cellar stairs satisfied the listener that he had not pulled it off intentionally.

She stood for a few moments, considering. It was a stout door and opened inwards. She took her bonnet from its nail in the kitchen and, walking softly to the street-door, set off to lay the case before a brother who lived a few doors away.

"Poor old Bill," said Mr. Cooper, when she had finished. "Still, it might be worse; he's got the barrel o' beer with him."

"It's not Bill," said Mrs. Simpson.

Mr. Cooper scratched his whiskers and looked at his wife.

"She ought to know," said the latter. "We'll come and have a look at him," said Mr. Cooper.

Mrs. Simpson pondered, and eyed him dubiously.

"Come in and have a bit of supper," she said at last. "There's a nice piece of beef and pickles."

"And Bill—I mean the stranger—sitting on the beer-barrel," said Mr. Cooper, gloomily.

"You can bring your beer with you," said his sister, sharply. "Come along."

Mr. Cooper grinned, and, placing a couple of bottles in his coat pockets, followed the two ladies to the house. Seated at the kitchen table, he grinned again, as a persistent drumming took place on the cellar door. His wife smiled, and a faint, sour attempt in the same direction appeared on the face of Mrs. Simpson.

"Open the door!" bellowed an indignant voice. "Open the door!"

Mrs. Simpson, commanding silence with an uplifted finger, proceeded to carve the beef. A rattle of knives and forks succeeded.

"O-pen-the-door!" said the voice again.

"Not so much noise," commanded Mr. Cooper. "I can't hear myself eat."

"Bob!" said the voice, in relieved accents, "Bob! Come and let me out."

Mr. Cooper, putting a huge hand over his mouth, struggled nobly with his feelings.

"Who are you calling 'Bob'?" he demanded, in an unsteady voice. "You keep yourself to yourself. I've heard all about you. You've got to stay there till my brother-in-law comes home."

"It's me, Bob," said Mr. Simpson—"Bill."

"Yes, I dare say," said Mr. Cooper; "but if you're Bill, why haven't you got Bill's voice?"

"Let me out and look at me," said Mr. Simpson.

There was a faint scream from both ladies, followed by protests.

"Don't be alarmed," said Mr. Cooper, reassuringly. "I wasn't born yesterday. I don't want to get a crack over the head."

"It's all a mistake, Bob," said the prisoner, appealingly. "I just had a shave and a haircut and—and a little hair-dye. If you open the door you'll know me at once."

"How would it be," said Mr. Cooper, turning to his sister, and speaking with unusual distinctness—"how would it be if you opened the door, and just as he put his head out I hit it a crack with the poker?"

"You try it on," said the voice behind the door, hotly. "You know who I am well enough, Bob Cooper. I don't want any more of your nonsense. Milly has put you up to this!"

"If your wife don't know you, how do you think I can?" said Mr. Cooper. "Now, look here; you keep quiet till my brother-in-law comes home. If he don't come home perhaps we shall be more likely to think you're him. If he's not home by to-morrow morning we—Hsh! Hsh! Don't you know there's ladies present?"

"That settles it," said Mrs. Cooper, speaking for the first time. "My brother-in-law would never talk like that."

"I should never forgive him if he did," said her husband, piously.

He poured himself out another glass of beer and resumed his supper with relish. Conversation turned on the weather, and from that to the price of potatoes. Frantic efforts on the part of the prisoner to join in the conversation and give it a more personal turn were disregarded. Finally he began to kick with monotonous persistency on the door.

"Stop it!" shouted Mr. Cooper.

"I won't," said Mr. Simpson.

The noise became unendurable. Mr. Cooper, who had just lit his pipe, laid it on the table and looked round at his companions.

"He'll have the door down soon," he said, rising. "Halloa, there!"

"Halloa!" said the other.

"You say you're Bill Simpson," said Mr. Cooper, holding up a forefinger at Mrs. Simpson, who was about to interrupt. "If you are, tell us something you know that only you could know; something we know, so as to identify you. Things about your past."

A strange noise sounded behind the door.

"Sounds as though he is smacking his lips," said Mrs. Cooper to her sister-in-law, who was eyeing Mr. Cooper restlessly.

"Very good," said Mr. Simpson; "I agree. Who is there?"

"Me and my wife and Mrs. Simpson," said Mr. Cooper.

"He is smacking his lips," whispered Mrs. Cooper. "Having a go at the beer, perhaps."

"Let's go back fifteen years," said Mr. Simpson in meditative tones. "Do you remember that girl with copper-coloured hair that used to live in John Street?"

"No!" said Mr. Cooper, loudly and suddenly.

"Do you remember coming to me one day—two days after Valentine Day, it was—white as chalk and shaking like a leaf, and—"

"NO!" roared Mr. Cooper.

"Very well, I must try something else, then," said Mr. Simpson, philosophically. "Carry your mind back ten years, Bob Cooper—"

"Look here!" said Mr. Cooper, turning round with a ghastly smile. "We'd better get off home, Mary. I don't like interfering in other people's concerns. Never did."

"You stay where you are," said his wife.

"Ten years," repeated the voice behind the door. "There was a new barmaid at the Crown, and one night you—"

"If I listen to any more of this nonsense I shall burst," remarked Mr. Cooper, plaintively.

"Go on," prompted Mrs. Cooper, grimly. "One night—"

"Never mind," said Mr. Simpson. "It doesn't matter. But does he identify me? Because if not I've got a lot more things I can try."

The harassed Mr. Cooper looked around appealingly.

"How do you expect me to recognize you—" he began, and stopped suddenly.

"Go back to your courting days, then," said Mr. Simpson, "when Mrs. Cooper wasn't Mrs. Cooper, but only wanted to be."

Mrs. Cooper shivered; so did Mr. Cooper.

"And you came round to me for advice," pursued Mr. Simpson, in reminiscent accents, "because there was another girl you wasn't sure of, and you didn't want to lose them both. Do you remember sitting with the two photographs—one on each knee—and trying to make up your mind?"

"Wonderful imagination," said Mr. Cooper, smiling in a ghastly fashion at his wife. "Hark at him!"

"I am harking," said Mrs. Cooper.

"Am I Bill Simpson or am I not?" demanded Mr. Simpson.

"Bill was always fond of his joke," said Mr. Cooper, with a glance at the company that would have moved an oyster. "He was always fond of making up things. You're like him in that. What do you think, Milly?"

"It's not my husband," said Mrs. Simpson.

"Tell us something about her," said Mr. Cooper, hastily.

"I daren't," said Mr. Simpson. "Doesn't that prove I'm her husband? But I'll tell you things about your wife, if you like."

"You dare!" said Mrs. Cooper, turning crimson, as she realized what confidences might have passed between husband and wife. "If you say a word of your lies about me, I don't know what I won't do to you."

"Very well, I must go on about Bob, then—till he recognizes me," said Mr. Simpson, patiently. "Carry your mind—"

"Open the door and let him out," shouted Mr. Cooper, turning to his sister. "How can I recognize a man through a deal door?"

Mrs. Simpson, after a little hesitation, handed him the key, and the next moment her husband stepped out and stood blinking in the gas-light.

"Do you recognize me?" he asked, turning to Mr. Cooper.

"I do," said that gentleman, with a ferocious growl.

"I'd know you anywhere," said Mrs. Cooper, with emphasis.

"And you?" said Mr. Simpson, turning to his wife.

"You're not my husband," she said, obstinately.

"Are you sure?" inquired Mr. Cooper.

"Certain."

"Very good, then," said her brother. "If he's not your husband I'm going to knock his head off for telling them lies about me."

He sprang forward and, catching Mr. Simpson by the collar, shook him violently until his head banged against the dresser. The next moment the hands of Mrs. Simpson were in the hair of Mr. Cooper.

"How dare you knock my husband about!" she screamed, as Mr. Cooper let go and caught her fingers. "You've hurt him."

"Concussion, I think," said Mr. Simpson, with great presence of mind.

His wife helped him to a chair and, wetting her handkerchief at the tap, tenderly bathed the dyed head. Mr. Cooper, breathing hard, stood by watching until his wife touched him on the arm.

"You come off home," she said, in a hard voice. "You ain't wanted. Are you going to stay here all night?"

"I should like to," said Mr. Cooper, wistfully.

STRIKING HARD

"You've what?" demanded Mrs. Porter, placing the hot iron carefully on its stand and turning a heated face on the head of the family.

"Struck," repeated Mr. Porter; "and the only wonder to me is we've stood it so long as we have. If I was to tell you all we've 'ad to put up with I don't suppose you'd believe me."

"Very likely," was the reply. "You can keep your fairy-tales for them that like 'em. They're no good to me."

"We stood it till flesh and blood could stand it no longer," declared her husband, "and at last we came out, shoulder to shoulder, singing. The people cheered us, and one of our leaders made 'em a speech."

"I should have liked to 'ave heard the singing," remarked his wife. "If they all sang like you, it must ha' been as good as a pantermime! Do you remember the last time you went on strike?"

"This is different," said Mr. Porter, with dignity.

"All our things went, bit by bit," pursued his wife, "all the money we had put by for a rainy day, and we 'ad to begin all over again. What are we going to live on? O' course, you might earn something by singing in the street; people who like funny faces might give you something! Why not go upstairs and put your 'ead under the bed-clothes and practise a bit?"

Mr. Porter coughed. "It'll be all right," he said, confidently. "Our committee knows what it's about; Bert Robinson is one of the best speakers I've ever 'eard. If we don't all get five bob a week more I'll eat my 'ead."

"It's the best thing you could do with it," snapped his wife. She took up her iron again, and turning an obstinate back to his remarks resumed her work.

Mr. Porter lay long next morning, and, dressing with comfortable slowness, noticed with pleasure that the sun was shining. Visions of a good breakfast and a digestive pipe, followed by a walk in the fresh air, passed before his eyes as he laced his boots. Whistling cheerfully he went briskly downstairs.

It was an October morning, but despite the invigorating chill in the air the kitchen-grate was cold and dull. Herring-bones and a disorderly collection of dirty cups and platters graced the table. Perplexed and angry, he looked around for his wife, and then, opening the back-door, stood gaping with astonishment. The wife of his bosom, who should have had a bright fire and a good breakfast waiting for him, was sitting on a box in the sunshine, elbows on knees and puffing laboriously at a cigarette.

"Susan!" he exclaimed.

Mrs. Porter turned, and, puffing out her lips, blew an immense volume of smoke. "Halloa!" she said, carelessly.

"Wot—wot does this mean?" demanded her husband.

Mrs. Porter smiled with conscious pride. "I made it come out of my nose just now," she replied. "At least, some of it did, and I swallowed the rest. Will it hurt me?"

"Where's my breakfast?" inquired the other, hotly. "Why ain't the kitchen-fire alight? Wot do you think you're doing of?"

"I'm not doing anything," said his wife, with an aggrieved air. "I'm on strike."

Mr. Porter reeled against the door-post. "Wot!" he stammered. "On strike? Nonsense! You can't be."

"O, yes, I can," retorted Mrs. Porter, closing one eye and ministering to it hastily with the corner of her apron. "Not 'aving no Bert Robinson to do it for me, I made a little speech all to myself, and here I am."

She dropped her apron, replaced the cigarette, and, with her hands on her plump knees, eyes him steadily.

"But—but this ain't a factory," objected the dismayed man; "and, besides —I won't 'ave it!"

Mrs. Porter laughed—a fat, comfortable laugh, but with a touch of hardness in it.

"All right, mate," she said, comfortably. "What are you out on strike for?"

"Shorter hours and more money," said Mr. Porter, glaring at her.

His wife nodded. "So am I," she said. "I wonder who gets it first?"

She smiled agreeably at the bewildered Mr. Porter, and, extracting a paper packet of cigarettes from her pocket, lit a fresh one at the stub of the first.

"That's the worst of a woman," said her husband, avoiding her eye and addressing a sanitary dustbin of severe aspect; "they do things without thinking first. That's why men are superior; before they do a thing they look at it all round, and upside down, and—and—make sure it can be done. Now, you get up in a temper this morning, and the first thing you do—not even waiting to get my breakfast ready first—is to go on strike. If you'd thought for two minutes you'd see as 'ow it's impossible for you to go on strike for more than a couple of hours or so."

"Why?" inquired Mrs. Porter.

"Kids," replied her husband, triumphantly. "They'll be coming 'ome from school soon, won't they? And they'll be wanting their dinner, won't they?"

"That's all right," murmured the other, vaguely.

"After which, when night comes," pursued Mr. Porter, "they'll 'ave to be put to bed. In the morning they'll 'ave to be got up and washed and dressed and given their breakfast and sent off to school. Then there's shopping wot must be done, and beds wot must be made."

"I'll make ours," said his wife, decidedly. "For my own sake."

"And wot about the others?" inquired Mr. Porter.

"The others'll be made by the same party as washes the children, and cooks their dinner for 'em, and puts 'em to bed, and cleans the 'ouse," was the reply.

"I'm not going to have your mother 'ere," exclaimed Mr. Porter, with sudden heat. "Mind that!"

"I don't want her," said Mrs. Porter. "It's a job for a strong, healthy man, not a pore old thing with swelled legs and short in the breath."

"Strong—'ealthy—man!" repeated her husband, in a dazed voice. "Strong—'eal—Wot are you talking about?"

Mrs. Porter beamed on him. "You," she said, sweetly.

There was a long silence, broken at last by a firework display of expletives. Mrs. Porter, still smiling, sat unmoved.

"You may smile!" raved the indignant Mr. Porter. "You may sit there smiling and smoking like a—like a man, but if you think that I'm going to get the meals ready, and soil my 'ands with making beds and washing-up, you're mistook. There's some 'usbands I know as would set about you!"

Mrs. Porter rose. "Well, I can't sit here gossiping with you all day," she said, entering the house.

"Wot are you going to do?" demanded her husband, following her.

"Going to see Aunt Jane and 'ave a bit o' dinner with her," was the reply. "And after that I think I shall go to the 'pictures.' If you 'ave bloaters for dinner be very careful with little Jemmy and the bones."

"I forbid you to leave this 'ouse !" said Mr. Porter, in a thrilling voice. "If you do you won't find nothing done when you come home, and all the kids dirty and starving."

"Cheerio!" said Mrs. Porter.

Arrayed in her Sunday best she left the house half an hour later. A glance over her shoulder revealed her husband huddled up in a chair in the dirty kitchen, gazing straight before him at the empty grate.

He made a hearty breakfast at a neighbouring coffee-shop, and, returning home, lit the fire and sat before it, smoking. The return of the four children from school, soon after midday, found him still wrestling with the difficulties of the situation. His announcement that their mother was out and that there would be no dinner was received at first in stupefied silence. Then Jemmy, opening his mouth to its widest extent, acted as conductor to an all-too-willing chorus.

The noise was unbearable, and Mr. Porter said so. Pleased with the tribute, the choir re-doubled its efforts, and Mr. Porter, vociferating orders for silence, saw only too clearly the base advantage his wife had taken of his affection for his children. He took some money from his pocket and sent the leading treble out marketing, after which, with the assistance of a soprano aged eight, he washed up the breakfast things and placed one of them in the dustbin.

The entire family stood at his elbow as he cooked the dinner, and watched, with bated breath, his frantic efforts to recover a sausage which had fallen out of the frying-pan into the fire. A fourfold sigh of relief heralded its return to the pan.

"Mother always—" began the eldest boy.

Mr. Porter took his scorched fingers out of his mouth and smacked the critic's head.

The dinner was not a success. Portions of half-cooked sausages returned to the pan, and coming back in the guise of cinders failed to find their rightful owners.

"Last time we had sausages," said the eight-year-old Muriel, "they melted in your mouth." Mr. Porter glowered at her.

"Instead of in the fire," said the eldest boy, with a mournful snigger.

"If I get up to you, my lad," said the harassed Mr. Porter, "you'll know it! Pity you don't keep your sharpness for your lessons! Wot country is Africa in?"

"Why, Africa's a continent!" said the startled youth.

"Jes so," said his father; "but wot I'm asking you is: wot country is it in?"

"Asia," said the reckless one, with a side-glance at Muriel.

"And why couldn't you say so before?" demanded Mr. Porter, sternly. "Now, you go to the sink and give yourself a thorough good wash. And mind you come straight home from school. There's work to be done."

He did some of it himself after the children had gone, and finished up the afternoon with a little shopping, in the course of which he twice changed his grocer and was threatened with an action for slander by his fishmonger. He returned home with his clothes bulging, although a couple of eggs in the left-hand coat-pocket had done their best to accommodate themselves to his figure.

He went to bed at eleven o'clock, and at a quarter past, clad all too lightly for the job, sped rapidly downstairs to admit his wife.

"Some 'usbands would 'ave let you sleep on the doorstep all night," he said, crisply.

"I know they would," returned his wife, cheerfully. "That's why I married you. I remember the first time I let you come 'ome with me, mother ses: 'There ain't much of 'im, Susan,' she ses; 'still, arf a loaf is better than—'"

The bedroom-door slammed behind the indignant Mr. Porter, and the three lumps and a depression which had once been a bed received his quivering frame again. With the sheet obstinately drawn over his head he turned a deaf ear to his wife's panegyrics on striking and her heartfelt tribute to the end of a perfect day. Even when standing on the cold floor while she remade the bed he maintained an attitude of unbending dignity, only relaxing when she smote him light-heartedly with the bolster. In a few ill-chosen words he expressed his opinion of her mother and her deplorable methods of bringing up her daughters.

He rose early next morning, and, after getting his own breakfast, put on his cap and went out, closing the street-door with a bang that awoke the entire family and caused the somnolent Mrs. Porter to open one eye for the purpose of winking with it. Slowly, as became a man of leisure, he strolled down to the works, and, moving from knot to knot of his colleagues, discussed the prospects of victory. Later on, with a little natural diffidence, he drew Mr. Bert Robinson apart and asked his advice upon a situation which was growing more and more difficult.

"I've got my hands pretty full as it is, you know," said Mr. Robinson, hastily.

"I know you 'ave, Bert," murmured the other. "But, you see, she told me last night she's going to try and get some of the other chaps' wives to join 'er, so I thought I ought to tell you."

Mr. Robinson started. "Have you tried giving her a hiding?" he inquired.

Mr. Porter shook his head. "I daren't trust myself," he replied. "I might go too far, once I started."

"What about appealing to her better nature?" inquired the other.

"She ain't got one," said the unfortunate. "Well, I'm sorry for you," said Mr. Robinson, "but I'm busy. I've got to see a Labour-leader this afternoon, and two reporters, and this evening there's the meeting. Try kindness first, and if that don't do, lock her up in her bedroom and keep her on bread and water."

He moved off to confer with his supporters, and Mr. Porter, after wandering aimlessly about for an hour or two, returned home at mid-day with a faint hope that his wife might have seen the error of her ways and provided dinner for him. He found the house empty and the beds unmade. The remains of breakfast stood on the kitchen-table, and a puddle of cold tea decorated the floor. The arrival of the children from school, hungry and eager, completed his discomfiture.

For several days he wrestled grimly with the situation, while Mrs. Porter, who had planned out her week into four days of charing, two of amusement, and Sunday in bed, looked on with smiling approval. She even offered to give him a little instruction—verbal—in scrubbing the kitchen-floor.

Mr. Porter, who was on his knees at the time, rose slowly to his full height, and, with a superb gesture, emptied the bucket, which also contained a scrubbing-brush and lump of soap, into the back-yard. Then he set off down the street in quest of a staff.

He found it in the person of Maudie Stevens, aged fourteen, who lived a few doors lower down. Fresh from school the week before, she cheerfully undertook to do the housework and cooking, and to act as nursemaid in her spare time. Her father, on his part, cheerfully under-took to take care of her wages for her, the first week's, payable in advance, being banked the same evening at the Lord Nelson.

It was another mouth to feed, but the strike-pay was coming in very well, and Mr. Porter, relieved from his unmanly tasks, walked the streets a free man. Beds were made without his interference, meals were ready (roughly) at the appointed hour, and for the first time since the strike he experienced satisfaction in finding fault with the cook. The children's content was not so great, Maudie possessing a faith in the virtues of soap and water that they made no attempt to share. They were greatly relieved when their mother returned home after spending a couple of days with Aunt Jane.

"What's all this?" she demanded, as she entered the kitchen, followed by a lady-friend.

"What's all what?" inquired Mr. Porter, who was sitting at dinner with the family.

"That," said his wife, pointing at the cook-general.

Mr. Porter put down his knife and fork. "Got 'er in to help," he replied, uneasily.

"Do you hear that?" demanded his wife, turning to her friend, Mrs. Gorman. "Oh, these masters!"

"Ah!" said her friend, vaguely.

"A strike-breaker!" said Mrs. Porter, rolling her eyes.

"Shame!" said Mrs. Gorman, beginning to understand.

"Coming after my job, and taking the bread out of my mouth," continued Mrs. Porter, fluently. "Underselling me too, I'll be bound. That's what comes of not having pickets."

"Unskilled labour," said Mrs. Gorman, tightening her lips and shaking her head.

"A scab!" cried Mrs. Porter, wildly. "A scab!"

"Put her out," counselled her friend.

"Put her out!" repeated Mrs. Porter, in a terrible voice. "Put her out! I'll tear her limb from limb! I'll put her in the copper and boil her!"

Her voice was so loud and her appearance so alarming that the unfortunate Maudie, emitting three piercing shrieks, rose hastily from the table and looked around for a way of escape. The road to the front-door was barred, and with a final yelp that set her employer's teeth on edge she dashed into the yard and went home via the back-fences. Housewives busy in their kitchens looked up in amazement at the spectacle of a pair of thin black legs descending one fence, scudding across the yard to the accompaniment of a terrified moaning, and scrambling madly over the other. At her own back-door Maudie collapsed on the step, and, to the intense discomfort and annoyance of her father, had her first fit of hysterics.

"And the next scab that comes into my house won't get off so easy," said Mrs. Porter to her husband. "D'you understand?"

"If you 'ad some husbands—" began Mr. Porter, trembling with rage.

"Yes, I know," said his wife, nodding. "Don't cry, Jemmy," she added, taking the youngest on her knee. "Mother's only having a little game. She and dad are both on strike for more pay and less work."

Mr. Porter got up, and without going through the formality of saying good-bye to the hard-featured Mrs. Gorman, put on his cap and went out. Over a couple of half-pints taken as a sedative, he realized the growing seriousness of his position.

In a dull resigned fashion he took up his household duties again, made harder now than before by the scandalous gossip of the aggrieved Mr. Stevens. The anonymous present of a much-worn apron put the finishing touch to his discomfiture; and the well-meant offer of a fair neighbour to teach him how to shake a mat without choking himself met with a reception that took her breath away.

It was a surprise to him one afternoon to find that his wife had so far unbent as to tidy up the parlour. Ornaments had been dusted and polished and the carpet swept. She had even altered the position of the furniture. The table had been pushed against the wall, and the easy-chair, with its back to the window, stood stiffly confronting six or seven assorted chairs, two of which at least had been promoted from a lower sphere.

"It's for the meeting," said Muriel, peeping in.

"Meeting?" repeated her father, in a dazed voice.

"Strike-meetings," was the reply. "Mrs. Gorman and some other ladies are coming at four o'clock. Didn't mother tell you?"

Mr. Porter, staring helplessly at the row of chairs, shook his head.

"Mrs. Evans is coming," continued Muriel, in a hushed voice—"the lady what punched Mr. Brown because he kept Bobbie Evans in one day. He ain't been kept in since. I wish you—"

She stopped suddenly, and, held by her father's gaze, backed slowly out of the room. Mr. Porter, left with the chairs, stood regarding them thoughtfully. Their emptiness made an appeal that no right-minded man could ignore. He put his hand over his mouth and his eyes watered.

He spent the next half-hour in issuing invitations, and at half-past three every chair was filled by fellow-strikers. Three cans of beer, clay pipes, and a paper of shag stood on the table. Mr. Benjamin Todd, an obese, fresh-coloured gentleman of middle age, took the easy-chair. Glasses and teacups were filled.

"Gentlemen," said Mr. Todd, lighting his pipe, "afore we get on to the business of this meeting I want to remind you that there is another meeting, of ladies, at four o'clock; so we've got to hurry up. O' course, if it should happen that we ain't finished—"

"Go on, Bennie!" said a delighted admirer. "I see a female 'ead peeping in at the winder already," said a voice.

"Let 'em peep," said Mr. Todd, benignly. "Then p'r'aps they'll be able to see how to run a meeting."

"There's two more 'eads," said the other. "Oh, Lord, I know I sha'n't be able to keep a straight face!"

"H'sh!" commanded Mr. Todd, sternly, as the street-door was heard to open. "Be'ave yourself. As I was saying, the thing we've got to consider about this strike—"

The door opened, and six ladies, headed by Mrs. Porter, entered the room in single file and ranged themselves silently along the wall.

"Strike," proceeded Mr. Todd, who found himself gazing uneasily into the eyes of Mrs. Gorman—"strike—er—strike—"

"He said that before," said a stout lady, in a loud whisper; "I'm sure he did."

"Is," continued Mr. Todd, "that we have got to keep this—this—er—"

"Strike," prompted the same voice.

Mr. Todd paused, and, wiping his mouth with a red pocket-handkerchief, sat staring straight before him.

"I move," said Mrs. Evans, her sharp features twitching with excitement, "that Mrs. Gorman takes the chair."

"'Ow can I take it when he's sitting in it?" demanded that lady.

"She's a lady that knows what she wants and how to get it," pursued Mrs. Evans, unheeding. "She understands men—"

"I've buried two 'usbands," murmured Mrs. Gorman, nodding.

"And how to manage them," continued Mrs. Evans. "I move that Mrs. Gorman takes the chair. Those in favour—"

Mr. Todd, leaning back in his chair and gripping the arms, gazed defiantly at a row of palms.

"Carried unanimously!" snapped Mrs. Evans.

Mrs. Gorman, tall and bony, advanced and stood over Mr. Todd. Strong men held their breath.

"It's my chair," she said, gruffly. "I've been moved into it."

"Possession," said Mr. Todd, in as firm a voice as he could manage, "is nine points of the law. I'm here and—"

Mrs. Gorman turned, and, without the slightest warning, sat down suddenly and heavily in his lap. A hum of admiration greeted the achievement.

"Get up!" shouted the horrified Mr. Todd. "Get up!"

Mrs. Gorman settled herself more firmly.

"Let me get up," said Mr. Todd, panting.

Mrs. Gorman rose, but remained in a hovering position, between which and the chair Mr. Todd, flushed and dishevelled, extricated himself in all haste. A shrill titter of laughter and a clapping of hands greeted his appearance. He turned furiously on the pallid Mr. Porter.

"What d'you mean by it?" he demanded. "Are you the master, or ain't you? A man what can't keep order in his own house ain't fit to be called a man. If my wife was carrying on like this—"

"I wish I was your wife," said Mrs. Gorman, moistening her lips.

Mr. Todd turned slowly and surveyed her.

"I don't," he said, simply, and, being by this time near the door, faded gently from the room.

"Order!" cried Mrs. Gorman, thumping the arm of her chair with a large, hard-working fist. "Take your seats, ladies."

A strange thrill passed through the bodies of her companions and communicated itself to the men in the chairs. There was a moment's tense pause, and then the end man, muttering something about "going to see what had happened to poor old Ben Todd," rose slowly and went out. His companions, with heads erect and a look of cold disdain upon their faces, followed him.

It was Mr. Porter's last meeting, but his wife had several more. They lasted, in fact, until the day, a fortnight later, when he came in with flushed face and sparkling eyes to announce that the strike was over and the men victorious.

"Six bob a week more!" he said, with enthusiasm. "You see, I was right to strike, after all."

Mrs. Porter eyed him. "I am out for four bob a week more," she said, calmly.

Her husband swallowed. "You—you don't understand 'ow these things are done," he said, at last. "It takes time. We ought to ne—negotiate."

"All right," said Mrs. Porter, readily. "Seven shillings a week, then."

"Let's say four and have done with it," exclaimed the other, hastily.

And Mrs. Porter said it.

THE SUBSTITUTE

The night watchman had just returned to the office fire after leaving it to attend a ring at the wharf bell. He sat for some time puffing fiercely at his pipe and breathing heavily.

"Boys!" he said, at last. "That's the third time this week, and yet if I was to catch one and skin 'im alive I suppose I should get into trouble over it. Even 'is own father and mother would make a fuss, most like. Some people have boys, and other people 'ave the trouble of 'em. Our street's full of 'em, and the way they carry on would make a monkey-'ouse ashamed of itself. The man next door to me's got seven of 'em, and when I spoke to 'im friendly about it over a pint one night, he put the blame on 'is wife.

"The worst boy I ever knew used to be office-boy in this 'ere office, and I can't understand now why I wasn't 'ung for him. Undersized little chap he was, with a face the colour o' bad pie-crust, and two little black eyes like shoe-buttons. To see 'im with his little white cuffs, and a stand-up collar, and a little black bow, and a little bowler-'at, was enough to make a cat laugh. I told 'im so one day, and arter that we knew where we was. Both of us.

"By rights he ought to 'ave left the office at six—just my time for coming on. As it was, he used to stay late, purtending to work 'ard so as to get a rise. Arter all the clerks 'ad gorn 'ome he used to sit perched up on a stool yards too 'igh for him, with one eye on the ledger and the other looking through the winder at me. I remember once going off for 'arf a pint, and when I come back I found 'im with a policeman, two carmen, and all the hands off of the Maid Marian, standing on the edge of the jetty, waiting for me to come up. He said that, not finding me on the wharf, 'e made sure that I must 'ave tumbled overboard, as he felt certain that I wouldn't neglect my dooty while there was breath in my body; but 'e was sorry to find 'e was mistook. He stood there talking like a little clergyman, until one of the carmen knocked his 'at over 'is eyes, and then he forgot 'imself for a bit.

"Arter that I used to wait until he 'ad gorn afore I 'ad my arf-pint. I didn't want my good name taken away, and I had to be careful, and many's the good arf-pint I 'ad to refuse because that little imitation monkey was sitting in the office drawing faces on 'is blotting-paper. But sometimes it don't matter 'ow careful you are, you make a mistake.

"There was a little steamer, called the Eastern Monarch, used to come up here in them days, once a week. Fat little tub she was, with a crew o' fattish old men, and a skipper that I didn't like. He'd been in the coasting trade all 'is life, while I've knocked about all over the world, but to hear 'im talk you'd think he knew more about things than I did.

"Eddication, Bill,' he ses one evening, 'that's the thing! You can't argufy without it; you only talk foolish, like you are doing now.'

"'There's eddication and there's common sense,' I ses. 'Some people 'as one and some people 'as the other. Give me common sense.'

"'That's wot you want,' he ses, nodding.

"'And, o' course,' I ses, looking at 'im, 'there's some people 'asn't got either one or the other.'

"The office-boy came out of the office afore he could think of an answer, and the pair of 'em stood there talking to show off their cleverness, till their tongues ached. I took up my broom and went on sweeping, and they was so busy talking long words they didn't know the meaning of to each other that they was arf choked with dust afore they noticed it. When they did notice it they left off using long words, and the skipper tried to hurt my feelings with a few short ones 'e knew.

"'It's no good wasting your breath on 'im,' ses the boy. 'You might as well talk to a beer-barrel.'

"He went off, dusting 'imself down with his little pocket-'ankercher, and arter the skipper 'ad told me wot he'd like to do, only he was too sorry for me to do it, 'e went back to the ship to put on a clean collar, and went off for the evening.

"He always used to go off by hisself of a evening, and I used to wonder 'ow he passed the time. Then one night I found out.

"I had just come out of the Bear's Head, and stopped to look round afore going back to the wharf, when I see a couple o' people standing on the swing-bridge saying 'Good-bye' to each other. One of 'em was a man and the other wasn't.

"'Evening, cap'n,' I ses, as he came towards me, and gave a little start. 'I didn't know you 'ad brought your missis up with you this trip.'

"'Evening, Bill,' he ses, very peaceful. 'Wot a lovely evening!'

"'Bee-utiful!' I ses.

"'So fresh,' ses the skipper, sniffing in some of the air.

"'Makes you feel quite young agin,' I ses.

"He didn't say nothing to that, except to look at me out of the corner of 'is eye; and stepping on to the wharf had another look at the sky to admire it, and then went aboard his ship. If he 'ad only stood me a pint, and trusted me, things might ha' turned out different.

"Quite by chance I happened to be in the Bear's Head a week arterwards, and, quite by chance, as I came out I saw the skipper saying 'Good-bye' on the bridge agin. He seemed to be put out about something, and when I said 'Wot a lovely evening it would be if only it wasn't raining 'ard!' he said something about knocking my 'ead off.

"'And you keep your nose out o' my bisness,' he ses, very fierce.

"'Your bisness!' I ses. 'Wot bisness?'

"'There's some people as might like to know that you leave the wharf to look arter itself while you're sitting in a pub swilling gallons and gallons o' beer,' he ses, in a nasty sort o' way. 'Live and let live, that's my motter."

"'I don't know wot you're talking about,' I ses, 'but it don't matter anyways. I've got a clear conscience; that's the main thing. I'm as open as the day, and there's nothing about me that I'd mind anybody knowing. Wot a pity it is everybody can't say the same!'

"I didn't see 'im saying 'Good-bye' the next week or the week arter that either, but the third week, arter just calling in at the Bear's Head, I strolled on casual-like and got as far as the bottom of Tower Hill afore I remembered myself. Turning the corner, I a'most fell over the skipper, wot was right in the fair way, shaking 'ands with his lady-friend under the lamp-post. Both of 'em started, and I couldn't make up my mind which gave me the most unpleasant look.

"'Peep-bo!' I ses, cheerful-like.

"He stood making a gobbling noise at me, like a turkey.

"'Give me quite a start, you did,' I ses. 'I didn't dream of you being there.'

"'Get off!' he ses, spluttering. 'Get off, afore I tear you limb from limb! 'Ow dare you follow me about and come spying round corners at me? Wot d'ye mean by it?'

"I stood there with my arms folded acrost my chest, as calm as a cucumber. The other party stood there watching us, and wot 'e could 'ave seen in her, I can't think. She was dressed more like a man than a woman, and it would have taken the good looks of twenty like her to 'ave made one barmaid. I stood looking at 'er like a man in a dream.

"'Well, will you know me agin?' she ses, in a nasty cracked sort of voice.

"'I could pick you out of a million,' I ses—'if I wanted to.'

"'Clear out!' ses the skipper. 'Clear out! And thank your stars there's a lady present.'

"'Don't take no notice of 'im, Captain Pratt,' ses the lady. 'He's beneath you. You only encourage people like that by taking notice of 'em. Good-bye.'

"She held out her 'and, and while the skipper was shaking it I began to walk back to the wharf. I 'adn't gorn far afore I heard 'im coming up behind me, and next moment 'e was walking alongside and saying things to try and make me lose my temper.

"'Ah, it's a pity your pore missis can't 'ear you!' I ses. 'I expect she thinks you are stowed away in your bunk dreaming of 'er, instead of saying things about a face as don't belong to you.'

"'You mind your bisness,' he ses, shouting. 'And not so much about my missis! D'ye hear? Wot's it got to do with you? Who asked you to shove your oar in?'

"'You're quite mistook,' I ses, very calm. 'I'd no idea that there was anything on as shouldn't be. I was never more surprised in my life. If anybody 'ad told me, I shouldn't 'ave believed 'em. I couldn't. Knowing you, and knowing 'ow respectable you 'ave always purtended to be, and also and likewise that you ain't no chicken—'

"I thought 'e was going to 'ave a fit. He 'opped about, waving his arms and stuttering and going on in such a silly way that I didn't like to be seen with 'im. Twice he knocked my 'at off, and arter telling him wot would 'appen if 'e did it agin, I walked off and left him.

"Even then 'e wasn't satisfied, and arter coming on to the wharf and following me up and down like a little dog, he got in front of me and told me some more things he 'ad thought of.

"'If I catch you spying on me agin,' he ses, 'you'll wish you'd never been born!'

"'You get aboard and 'ave a quiet sleep,' I ses. 'You're wandering in your mind.'

"'The lady you saw me with,' he ses, looking at me very fierce, 'is a friend o' mine that I meet sometimes for the sake of her talk.'

"'Talk!' I ses, staring at 'im. 'Talk! Wot, can't one woman talk enough for you? Is your missis dumb? or wot?'

"'You don't understand,' he ses, cocking up 'is nose at me. 'She's a interleckshal woman; full of eddication and information. When my missis talks, she talks about the price o' things and says she must 'ave more money. Or else she talks about things I've done, or sometimes things I 'aven't done. It's all one to her. There's no pleasure in that sort o' talk. It don't help a man.'

"'I never 'eard of any talk as did,' I ses.

"'I don't suppose you did,' he ses, sneering-like. 'Now, to-night, fust of all, we talked about the House of Lords and whether it ought to be allowed; and arter that she gave me quite a little lecture on insecks.'

"'It don't seem proper to me,' I ses. 'I 'ave spoke to my wife about 'em once or twice, but I should no more think of talking about such things to a single lady—'

"He began to jump about agin as if I'd bit 'im, and he 'ad so much to say about my 'ed and blocks of wood that I pretty near lost my temper. I should ha' lost it with some men, but 'e was a very stiff-built chap and as hard as nails.

"'Beer's your trouble,' he ses, at last. 'Fust of all you put it down, and then it climbs up and soaks wot little brains you've got. Wot you want is a kind friend to prevent you from getting it.'

"I don't know wot it was, but I 'ad a sort of sinking feeling inside as 'e spoke, and next evening, when I saw 'im walk to the end of the jetty with the office-boy and stand there talking to 'im with his 'and on his shoulder, it came on worse than ever. And I put two and two together when the guv'nor came up to me next day, and, arter talking about 'dooty' and 'ow easy it was to get night-watchmen, mentioned in 'a off-'and sort of way that, if I left the wharf at all between six and six, I could stay away altogether.

"I didn't answer 'im a word. I might ha' told 'im that there was plenty of people arter me ready to give me double the money, but I knew he could never get anybody to do their dooty by the wharf like I 'ad done, so I kept quiet. It's the way I treat my missis nowadays, and it pays; in the old days I used to waste my breath answering 'er back.

"I wouldn't ha' minded so much if it 'adn't ha' been for that boy. He used to pass me, as 'e went off of a evening, with a little sly smile on 'is ugly little face, and sometimes when I was standing at the gate he'd give a sniff or two and say that he could smell beer, and he supposed it came from the Bear's Head.

"It was about three weeks arter the guv'nor 'ad forgot 'imself, and I was standing by the gate one evening, when I saw a woman coming along carrying a big bag in her 'and. I 'adn't seen 'er afore, and when she stopped in front of me and smiled I was on my guard at once. I don't smile at other people, and I don't expect them to smile at me.

"'At last!' she ses, setting down 'er bag and giving me another smile. 'I thought I was never going to get 'ere."

"I coughed and backed inside a little bit on to my own ground. I didn't want to 'ave that little beast of a office-boy spreading tales about me.

"'I've come up to 'ave a little fling,' she ses, smiling away harder than ever. 'My husband don't know I'm 'ere. He thinks I'm at 'ome.'

"I think I went back pretty near three yards.

"'I come up by train,' she ses, nodding.

"'Yes,' I ses, very severe, 'and wot about going back by it?'

"'Oh, I shall go back by ship,' she ses. 'Wot time do you expect the Eastern Monarch up?'

"'Well,' I ses, 'ardly knowing wot to make of 'er, 'she ought to be up this tide; but there's no reckoning on wot an old washtub with a engine like a sewing-machine inside 'er will do.'

"'Oh, indeed!' she ses, leaving off smiling very sudden. 'Oh, indeed! My husband might 'ave something to say about that.'

"'Your 'usband?' I ses.

"'Captain Pratt,' she ses, drawing 'erself up. 'I'm Mrs. Pratt. He left yesterday morning, and I've come up 'ere by train to give 'im a little surprise.'

"You might ha' knocked me down with a feather, and I stood there staring at her with my mouth open, trying to think.

"'Take care,' I ses at last. 'Take care as you don't give 'im too much of a surprise!'

"'Wot do you mean?' she ses, firing up.

"'Nothing,' I ses. 'Nothing, only I've known 'usbands in my time as didn't like being surprised—that's all. If you take my advice, you'll go straight back home agin.'

"'I'll tell 'im wot you say,' she ses, 'as soon as 'is ship comes in.'

"That's a woman all over; the moment they get into a temper they want to hurt somebody; and I made up my mind at once that, if anybody was going to be 'urt, it wasn't me. And, besides, I thought it might be for the skipper's good—in the long run.

"I broke it to her as gentle as I could. I didn't tell 'er much, I just gave her a few 'ints. Just enough to make her ask for more.

"'And mind,' I ses, 'I don't want to be brought into it. If you should 'appen to take a fancy into your 'ed to wait behind a pile of empties till the ship comes in, and then slip out and foller your 'usband and give 'im the little surprise you spoke of, it's nothing to do with me.'

"'I understand,' she ses, biting her lip. 'There's no need for 'im to know that I've been on the wharf at all.'

"I gave 'er a smile—I thought she deserved it—but she didn't smile back. She was rather a nice-looking woman in the ordinary way, but I could easy see 'ow temper spoils a woman's looks. She stood there giving little shivers and looking as if she wanted to bite somebody.

"'I'll go and hide now,' she ses.

"'Not yet,' I ses. 'You'll 'ave to wait till that little blackbeetle in the office 'as gorn.' 'Blackbeetle?' she ses, staring.

"'Office-boy,' I ses. 'He'd better not see you at all. S'pose you go off for a bit and come back when I whistle?'

"Afore she could answer the boy came out of the office, ready to go 'ome. He gave a little bit of a start when 'e saw me talking to a lady, and then 'e nips down sudden, about a couple o' yards away, and begins to do 'is bootlace up. It took 'im some time, because he 'ad to undo it fust, but 'e finished it at last, and arter a quick look at Mrs. Pratt, and one at me that I could ha' smacked his 'ed for, 'e went off whistling and showing 'is little cuffs.

"I stepped out into the road and watched 'im out o' sight. Then I told Mrs. Pratt to pick up 'er bag and foller me.

"As it 'appened there was a big pile of empties in the corner of the ware'ouse wall, just opposite the Eastern Monarch's berth. It might ha' been made for the job, and, arter I 'ad tucked her away behind and given 'er a box to sit on, I picked up my broom and began to make up for lost time.

"She sat there as quiet as a cat watching a mouse'ole, and I was going on with my work, stopping every now and then to look and see whether the Monarch was in sight, when I 'appened to turn round and see the office-boy standing on the edge of the wharf with his back to the empties, looking down at the water. I nearly dropped my broom.

""Ullo!' I ses, going up to 'im. 'I thought you 'ad gorn 'ome.'

"'I was going,' he ses, with a nasty oily little smile, 'and then it struck me all of a sudden 'ow lonely it was for you all alone 'ere, and I come back to keep you company.'

"He winked at something acrost the river as 'e spoke, and I stood there thinking my 'ardest wot was the best thing to be done. I couldn't get Mrs. Pratt away while 'e was there; besides which I felt quite sartain she wouldn't go. The only 'ope I 'ad was that he'd get tired of spying on me and go away before he found out she was 'iding on the wharf.

"I walked off in a unconcerned way—not too far—and, with one eye on 'im and the other on where Mrs. Pratt was 'iding, went on with my work. There's nothing like 'ard work when a man is worried, and I was a'most forgetting my troubles, when I looked up and saw the Monarch coming up the river.

"She turned to come into 'er berth, with the skipper shouting away on the bridge and making as much fuss as if 'e was berthing a liner. I helped to make 'er fast, and the skipper, arter 'e had 'ad a good look round to see wot 'e could find fault with, went below to clean 'imself.

"He was up agin in about ten minutes, with a clean collar and a clean face, and a blue neck-tie that looked as though it 'ad got yeller measles. Good temper 'e was in, too, and arter pulling the office-boy's ear, gentle, as 'e was passing, he stopped for a moment to 'ave a word with 'im.

"'Bit late, ain't you?' he ses.

"'I've been keeping a eye on the watchman,' ses the boy. 'He works better when 'e knows there's somebody watching 'im.'

"'Look 'ere!' I ses. 'You take yourself off; I've had about enough of you. You take your little face 'ome and ask your mother to wipe its nose. Strickly speaking, you've no right to be on the wharf at all at this time.'

"'I've as much right as other people,' he ses, giving me a wicked look. 'I've got more right than some people, p'r'aps.'

"He stooped down deliberate and, picking up a bit o' coke from the 'eap by the crane, pitched it over at the empties.

"'Stop that!' I ses, shouting at 'im.

"'What for?' 'e ses, shying another piece. 'Why shouldn't I?'

"'Cos I won't 'ave it,' I ses. 'D'ye hear? Stop it!'

"I rushed at 'im as he sent another piece over, and for the next two or three minutes 'e was dodging me and chucking coke at the empties, with the fool of a skipper standing by laughing, and two or three of the crew leaning over the side and cheering 'im on.

"'All right,' he ses, at last, dusting 'is hands together. 'I've finished. There's no need to make such a fuss over a bit of coke.'

"'You've wasted pretty near arf a 'undered-weight,' I ses. 'I've a good mind to report you.'

"'Don't do that, watchman!' he ses, in a pitiful voice. 'Don't do that! 'Ere, I tell you wot I'll do. I'll pick it all up agin.'

"Afore I could move 'and or foot he 'ad shifted a couple o' cases out of 'is way and was in among the empties. I stood there dazed-like while two bits o' coke came flying back past my 'ed; then I 'eard a loud whistle, and 'e came out agin with 'is eyes rolling and 'is mouth wide open.

"'Wot's the matter?' ses the skipper, staring at 'im.

"'I—I—I'm sorry, watchman,' ses that beast of a boy, purtending 'e was 'ardly able to speak. 'I'd no idea—'

"'All right,' I ses, very quick.

"'Wot's the matter?' ses the skipper agin; and as 'e spoke it came over me like a flash wot a false persition I was in, and wot a nasty-tempered man 'e could be when 'e liked.

"'Why didn't you tell me you'd got a lady-friend there?' ses the boy, shaking his 'ed at me. 'Why, I might 'ave hit 'er with a bit o' coke, and never forgiven myself!'

"'Lady-friend!' ses the skipper, with a start. 'Oh, Bill, I am surprised!'

"My throat was so dry I couldn't 'ardly speak. 'It's my missis,' I ses, at last.

"'Your missis?' ses the skipper. 'Woes she 'iding behind there for?'

"'She—she's shy,' I ses. 'Always was, all 'er life. She can't bear other people. She likes to be alone with me.'

"'Oh, watchman!' ses the boy. 'I wonder where you expect to go to?'

"'Missis my grandmother!' ses the skipper, with a wink. 'I'm going to 'ave a peep.'

"'Stand back!' I ses, pushing 'im off. 'I don't spy on you, and I don't want you to come spying on me. You get off! D'ye hear me? Get off!'

"We had a bit of a struggle, till my foot slipped, and while I was waving my arms and trying to get my balance back 'e made a dash for the empties. Next moment he was roaring like a mad bull that 'ad sat down in a sorsepan of boiling water, and rushing back agin to kill me.

"I believe that if it 'adn't ha' been for a couple o' lightermen wot 'ad just come on to the jetty from their skiff, and two of his own 'ands, he'd ha' done it. Crazy with passion 'e was, and it was all the four of 'em could do to hold 'im. Every now and then he'd get a yard nearer to me, and then they'd pull 'im back a couple o' yards and beg of 'im to listen to reason and 'ear wot I 'ad to say. And as soon as I started and began to tell 'em about 'is lady-friend he broke out worse than ever. People acrost the river must ha' wondered wot was 'appening. There was two lightermen, two sailormen, me and the skipper, and Mrs. Pratt all talking at once, and nobody listening but the office-boy. And in the middle of it all the wicket was pushed open and the 'ed of the lady wot all the trouble was about peeped in, and drew back agin.

"'There you are!' I ses, shouting my 'ardest. 'There she is. That's the lady I was telling you about. Now, then: put 'em face to face and clear my character. Don't let 'er escape.'

"One o' the lightermen let go o' the skipper and went arter 'er, and, just as I was giving the other three a helping 'and, 'e came back with 'er. Mrs. Pratt caught 'er breath, and as for the skipper, 'e didn't know where to look, as the saying is. I just saw the lady give 'im one quick look, and then afore I could dream of wot was coming, she rushes up to me and flings 'er long, bony arms round my neck.

"'Why, William!' she ses, 'wot's the matter? Why didn't you meet me? Didn't you get my letter? Or 'ave you ceased to care for me?"

"'Let go!' I ses, struggling. 'Let go! D'ye 'ear? Wot d'ye mean by it? You've got 'old of the wrong one.'

"'Oh, 'William!' she ses, arf strangling me. "'Ow can you talk to me like that? Where's your 'art?'

"I never knew a woman so strong. I don't suppose she'd ever 'ad the chance of getting 'er arms round a man's neck afore, and she hung on to me as if she'd never let go. And all the time I was trying to explain things to them over 'er shoulder I could see they didn't believe a word I was saying. One o' the lightermen said I was a 'wonder,' and the other said I was a 'fair cough-drop.' Me!

"She got tired of it at last, but by that time I was so done up I couldn't say a word. I just dropped on to a box and sat there getting my breath back while the skipper forgave 'is wife for 'er unjust suspicions of 'im—but told 'er not to do it agin—and the office-boy was saying I'd surprised even 'im. The last I saw of the lady-friend, the two lightermen was helping 'er to walk to the gate, and the two sailormen was follering 'er up behind, carrying 'er pocket-'ankercher and upberella."

W.W. Jacobs – A Short Biography

William Wymark Jacobs was born on September 8, 1863 in the Wapping district of London, England. An author, humorist and dramatist, Jacobs is best remembered for the enduring classic tale of horror - "The Monkey's Paw".

As a youth, Jacobs grew up near the Wapping docks in London, where his father was a wharf manager. The family's first home was home was a house on a River Thames wharf.

The docklands setting would show up frequently in his later literary output. Jacobs, the wharf rat, and his three siblings lost their mother when they were all still young children. Their father, William Gage Jacobs, remarried and fathered a further seven children with his erstwhile housekeeper Ellen Florey. Although he grew up surrounded by poverty, Jacobs himself received a formal education in London, first at a private prep school and later at the Birkbeck Literary and Scientific Institute (now part of the University of London and known as Birkbeck College).

Jacobs' adult working life began with a clerical position at the Post Office Savings Bank. The job was not a stimulating one but Jacobs put his imagination to good use and started to write short stories, sketches and articles, many of which appeared in the Post Office house publication "Blackfriars Magazine."

Although Jacobs did receive his fair share of rejection slips at the beginning of his career, many works written during this period of clerical employment appeared in the "Idler" and "Today" magazines, both of which were edited by noted humorist Jerome K. Jerome, who had taken a liking to Jacobs' stories.

From 1898, Jacobs also published stories in "The Strand", a popular, monthly fiction and general interest magazine. The arrangement stayed in place for most of his life and many of the works in Jacobs' subsequent collections – including the nautical serialization A Master of Craft (1899-1900) - appeared there first.

Jacobs' first volume of collected works was published in 1896. Many Cargoes, a selection of sea-faring yarns, established Jacobs as a popular writer and humorist with a penchant for authentic dialogue and trick endings (critics of the day referred to him as the "O. Henry of the Waterfront").

A year later he published a novelette, The Skipper's Wooing, and in 1898 and another collection of short stories titled Sea Urchins. These works painted vivid, if imaginatively stretched, pictures of dockland and seafaring London with colourful characters (such as "The Night Watchman", Ginger Dick) that now seem archetypal.

Many of Jacobs' periodical publications and first editions were illustrated with woodcuts and ink drawings, as was still the custom at the turn of the 20th century. The author worked regularly with artists such as E.W. Kemble, who had illustrated Mark Twain's Adventures of Huckleberry Finn and Harriet Beecher Stowe's Uncle Tom's Cabin, and his good friend Will Owen, who eventually became a household name on the strength of his iconic Bisto Kids, Bovril and Lux Soap advertising posters.

By 1899, Jacobs was able to quit the post office and finally begin a career making a living as a full-time writer.

He married the noted suffragist Agnes Eleanor Williams (who had been jailed for her protest activities) in 1900. They set up a household in Loughton, Essex as well as living part of the year in central London. The couple went on to have five children together though their marriage was considered an unhappy one.

The publication of two short novels: At Sunwich Port (a romantic tale of rival sea captains in the fictional seaside community of Sunwich standing in for the actual East England community of Sandwich, Kent) and Dialstone Lane (another small town romance involving intrigue and buried treasure), in 1902 and 1904 respectively, cemented Jacobs' reputation as one of the leading British authors of the new century.

On the foundations of a continuing ability to write for his audience he was readily published though he never strayed too far from what was becoming his familiar, dependable style. There followed a string of further successful publications, including Captain's All (1905), Night Watches (1914), The Castaways (1916), and Sea Whispers (1926). Jacobs published eighteen books in all during his lifetime; thirteen collections and five novels.

As a storyteller, Jacobs is perhaps better remembered for a handful of brief tales of the supernatural than for his popular nautical-themed works. The most famous of these, The Monkey's Paw, originally appeared as part of the 1902 short story collection The Lady of the Barge. It is an economically written story about a shriveled talisman, a monkey's paw that brings grief and horror in the wake of all too literal wish granting. The story has been adapted for other media repeatedly, starting with a one-act play performed at London's Haymarket Theatre in 1903. There have been multiple film adaptations of the story in the modern era; some of us are familiar with its appearance in an episode of the popular animated series, The Simpsons.

Another macabre gem, The Toll-House, was published as part of the collection Sailor's Knots in 1909. Jacob's once again employs a sparse style to tell the story of a group of men who spend the night in a famously haunted house on a dare (a noticeably similar narrative concept was put to use in the much earlier play The Ghost of Jerry Bundler, which had launched Jacobs' parallel career as a dramatist back in 1899 when it was produced at the St. James Theatre in London). Innovative at the time of writing, these sparingly written, atmospheric ghost stories are now familiar classics of the supernatural genre.

Though prolific in his younger years, Jacobs' productivity dropped dramatically after the start of World War I. Yet even in self-imposed semi-retirement Jacobs was still recognized as a leading humorist, ranked alongside such writers as P. G. Wodehouse and George Birmingham. He enjoyed continuing influence and elevated status among his fellow writers as evidenced by these comments attributed to his colleague Henry James:

"Mr. Jacobs, I envy you. You are popular! Your admirable work is appreciated by a wide circle of readers; it has achieved popularity. Mine never goes into a second edition."

James' literary fortunes would, of course, change, but his back-handedly complimentary admiration is compelling evidence of Jacobs' reputation as a writer and humourist both for his audience and his perhaps more admired literary colleagues.

Though Jacobs would create little in the way of new work after 1911, he was still writing. In these later years, seemingly burnt out creatively, Jacobs concentrated more on writing dramatizations and adaptations of his existing stories, including Beauty and the Barge (a film version starring Margaret Rutherford was also released in 1937) and In the Dark (a one act play that is often performed pr published with The Monkey's Paw adaptation).

Though admired by loyal readers throughout his lifetime, Jacobs has been almost completely forgotten since. Critics are at a loss to name a single reason why - Jacobs is universally considered to be a fine and imaginative literary craftsman. But, as critic John Wain suggested in a 1960 essay, perhaps Jacobs' humour may have been too gentle to persist into the cruel and sarcastic modern era, his dry pokes at proletariat hardship no longer suiting the times.

Nonetheless, Jacobs' legacy remains solid: he continued Dickens' (a writer with whom he is also often compared) tradition for sharing working class stories in authentic vernacular. And polished narratives such as The Monkey's Paw set a standard for the clever use of horror in fiction and popular culture that endures to this day. Indeed recently his works have begun to show an increased demand and appreciation in a world that is constantly looking over its shoulder.

William Wymark Jacobs died in a North London nursing home in Hornsey Lane, Islington on September 1st, 1943, just a week before his 80th birthday.

W.W. Jacobs – A Concise Bibliography

NOVELS AND SHORT STORY COLLECTIONS
MANY CARGOES (SHORT STORIES) (1896)
THE SKIPPER'S WOOING (1897)
SEA URCHINS (SHORT STORIES) (1898) aka MORE CARGOES
A MASTER OF CRAFT (1900)
LIGHT FREIGHTS (SHORT STORIES) (1901)
THE LADY OF THE BARGE (SHORT STORIES) (1902)
AT SUNWICH PORT (1902)
DIALSTONE LANE (1902)
SALTHAVEN (1908)
CAPTAINS ALL (SHORT STORIES) (1911)
NIGHT WATCHERS (SHORT STORIES) (1914)
DEEP WATERS (SHORT STORIES) (1919)

SHORT STORIES (INCLUDING THOSE USED IN THE COLLECTIONS ABOVE)
A BENEFIT PERFORMANCE
A BLACK AFFAIR
A CASE OF DESERTION
A CHANGE OF TREATMENT
A CIRCULAR TOUR
A DISCIPLINARIAN
A DISTANT RELATIVE
A GARDEN PLOT
A GOLDEN VENTURE
A HARBOUR OF REFUGE
A LOVE KNOT
A LOVE PASSAGE
A MARKED MAN
A MIXED PROPOSAL
A RASH EXPERIMENT
A SAFETY MATCH
A SPIRIT OF AVARICE
A TIGER'S SKIN
ADMIRAL PETERS
AFTER THE INQUEST
ALF'S DREAM
AN ADULTERATION ACT

THE TEMPTATION OF SAMUEL BURGE
THE TEST
THE THREE SISTERS
TO HAVE AND TO HOLD
"THE TOLL-HOUSE"
TWIN SPIRITS
TWO OF A TRADE
THE UNDERSTUDY
THE UNKNOWN
THE VIGIL
WATCH-DOGS
THE WEAKER VESSEL
THE WELL
THE WHITE CAT

STAGE
THE GHOST OF JERRY BUNDLER (1899) (In London)

FILM ADAPTATIONS
A MASTER OF CRAFT (1922)
THE MONKEY'S PAW (1933)
OUR RELATIONS, a Laurel & Hardy film, "suggested by" to Jacobs' "The Money Box." (1936)
FOOTSTEPS IN THE FOG, from the short story The Interruption. (1955)

www.ingramcontent.com/pod-product-compliance
Lightning Source LLC
Chambersburg PA
CBHW071330130626
46556CB00004B/1830